CONJUGAL LOVE

Also by Alberto Moravia

FICTION

THE WOMAN OF ROME
THE CONFORMIST
TWO ADOLESCENTS
(*Agostino* and *Disobedience*)
THE FANCY DRESS PARTY
THE TIME OF INDIFFERENCE
ROMAN TALES
A GHOST AT NOON
BITTER HONEYMOON
TWO WOMEN
THE WAYWARD WIFE
THE EMPTY CANVAS
MORE ROMAN TALES
THE FETISH
THE LIE
COMMAND AND I WILL OBEY YOU
PARADISE
THE TWO OF US

GENERAL

MAN AS AN END
THE RED BOOK AND THE GREAT WALL

PLAY

BEATRICE CENCI

CONJUGAL LOVE

ALBERTO MORAVIA

Translated from the Italian
by
ANGUS DAVIDSON

SECKER & WARBURG
LONDON

Originally published in Italian as *L'Amore Coniugale*

First published in England 1951 by
Martin Secker & Warburg Limited
14 Carlisle Street, London W1V 6NN

Copyright © 1949 by Casa Editrice Valentino Bompiani

English translation copyright ©
Martin Secker & Warburg Limited 1951

Reprinted 1951
Reprinted 1952
Re-issued 1974

SBN 436 28552 5

100 284888

Printed in Great Britain by
REDWOOD BURN LIMITED
Trowbridge & Esher

FIRST of all I wish to speak of my wife. Loving, apart from many other things, means taking a delight in looking at and watching the loved one. Taking a delight, that is to say, in contemplating not merely the beauties but also the defects, whether they be few or many, of that person. From the very first days of our married life, I found an inestimable pleasure in looking at Leda (that is her name), and in studying even the most insignificant and fleeting movements and expressions of her face and body. My wife, at the time we were married (later, after she had borne three children, certain of her characteristics were, I do not say changed, but to some extent modified) was just over thirty years old. She was, if not exactly tall, above the middle height; and her face and figure were both very beautiful, though far from perfect. Her long, thin face had a withdrawn, dazed, almost obliterated look, like that of a classical deity in some old picture of mediocre quality in which the vagueness of the painting is increased by the patina of age. This strange look of intangible beauty which, like a gleam of sunshine on a wall or the shadow of a cloud passing over the sea, might vanish at any moment, came without doubt partly from her hair, which was of a metallic fairness and always a little untidy with long trailing locks that seemed to suggest a flutter of fear or flight, and partly from her blue eyes, which were enormous and slightly slanting, with dilated, glistening pupils whose troubled, evasive glance suggested, as did her hair, a state of mind both frightened and shy. Her nose was large and straight and nobly formed, her wide red mouth unusually sinuous in shape, and with a look of surly, heavy sensuality, the lower lip curving deeply back over a chin which was too small. It was an irregular face, but nevertheless a very beautiful one, with, as I have already said, an intangible beauty which at certain moments and in certain circumstances, as I shall explain later, seemed to dissolve and disappear. The same might be said of her body. From the waist upwards she was as slim and delicate as a young girl; on the other hand her hips, her belly, her legs, were solid, strong, adult, full of muscular energy and swagger. But this lack of harmony, like the lack of harmony in her face, was neutralized by the beauty which enveloped her from head to foot, in a halo of perfection, as though it were an impalpable attendant aura or a mysteriously transfiguring light. Strange to say, sometimes, as I looked at her, I actually thought of her as a person of classical form and features, without defects, all harmony and serenity and symmetry: to such an extent did this beauty, which for want of other words I am compelled to call spiritual, beguile and seduce me. But there were moments when the golden veil was torn, and then not only were the many irregularities revealed to me but I was also witness of a painful transformation of her whole personality.

I made this discovery during the first days of our married life and for a moment I had almost the feeling of having been deceived, like a man who, having married for money, discovers after the wedding that his wife is poor. For, at times, my wife's whole face would be twisted into a heavy, mute grimace in which fear, anguish and waywardness all seemed to be expressed, and, at the same time, an unwilling sexual attraction. This grimace would cause the natural irregularity of her features to leap to the eye, so to speak, in a most violent manner, giving her whole face the repellent appearance of a grotesque mask in which, for the sake of a particular comic quality, partly obscene and partly painful, certain features had been deliberately exaggerated, to the point of caricature: the mouth especially, and also the two lines at the sides of the mouth, and the nostrils and the eyes. My wife had the habit of painting her lips heavily, with scarlet lipstick; and also, being pale, she used to put rouge on her cheeks. These artificial colours were not noticeable when the expression of her face was calm, since they harmonized with the colour of her eyes, of her hair and complexion. But when she grimaced, they stood out, crude and flaming, and her face, which a moment before had been so serene, so luminous, so classically beautiful, brought to mind the ridiculous highly-coloured features of a carnival mask. And to this there was added that touch of obscenity that such physical distortions acquire from the softness and warmth of living flesh.

Similarly her body, like her face, had a way of putting to flight the enchanted air of beauty, of performing ugly contortions. She would crumple up completely, as though in fear or disgust; but at the same time, like a certain kind of dancer or mime whose aim is to excite her audience, while her arms and legs were thrust forward in an attitude of defence or aversion, her body would

7

bend backwards in an inviting, provoking posture. She would indeed appear to be thrusting away some imaginary danger, and yet, at the same moment, to be indicating by that vehement twisting of her hips that the danger or assault was not unwelcome. It was a graceless attitude and, accompanied as it sometimes was by the facial grimace, it made one doubt, almost, whether one was still face to face with the same person who, a moment before, had been so composed, so serene, so unspeakably lovely.

I have said that loving means loving everything about the beloved person, the defects, if there are any, just as much as the beauties. These grimaces, these distortions, although extremely ugly, were soon just as dear to me as the beauty, the harmony, the serenity of the better moments. But loving, sometimes, also means not understanding; for if it is true that there is one form of love that implies full comprehension, it is also true that there is another, more passionate, form that makes one blind with regard to the loved one. I was not exactly blind; but I lacked the mental lucidity of a tested, long-standing love. I knew that my wife, in certain circumstances, became ugly and graceless; this seemed to me a curious fact and, like everything else about her, lovable; but beyond the establishment of the fact I was neither able, nor did I wish, to go.

I ought, at this point, to say that the grimace and the distortion occurred very rarely and never at intimate moments in our relationship. I do not remember any word or gesture of mine ever producing that strange transmutation of her face into a mask or of her body into a marionette. On the contrary, in our moments of love-making she seemed to achieve the highest degree of that unbelievable, unspeakable beauty of hers. At such times the dilated, moist pupils of her great eyes held a troubled appeal that was gentle and sweet and more expressive than any speech; her mouth seemed to proclaim, through the sensuality and the sinuosity of her lips, a capricious, intelligent kindness all its own; and her whole face welcomed my gaze like a mysterious but reassuring mirror to which the fair, tousled hair made a worthy frame. Her body too seemed then to fall into its loveliest shape, lying there innocent and languid, without strength and without shame, like a promised land that displayed itself to the first glance all open and golden, with its fields and its rivers, its hills and its valleys, to the furthest horizon. The grimace and the distortions, on the other hand, were produced by the most unexpected and unimportant circumstances; it will be enough if I mention just a few of them. My wife has always been a great reader of detective stories. I noticed that, when she reached the point where the plot became most en-thralling and most frightening, her face would gradually twist itself into that grimace; and it would not disappear again until the end of the passage that had induced it. My wife was likewise very fond of gambling. I was with her at Campione, at Monte Carlo, at San Remo: and every single time, after she had made her stake, while the wheel was going round and the little ball jumping from number to number, her face would take on that ugly grimace. Finally, even the act of inserting a piece of thread into the eye of a needle sufficed to make her grimace; or a

9

child running along the edge of a brook at the risk of falling in; or even a drop of cold water down her back.

I want, however, to mention at greater length two cases in which it seemed to me that this strange transformation of hers had more complicated origins. One day we happened to be in the garden of our country villa and I was struggling to pull up a tall, overgrown weed, almost a bush, which, goodness knows how, had grown up in the middle of the open space in front of the house. It was not easy, because the green, moist plant was slippery to my grasp and also, obviously, had very deep roots. While intent on this operation, for some reason I raised my eyes in the direction of my wife and was astonished to see that both her face and body were completely transformed by the usual ugly grimace and contortion. At the same moment the plant, yielding to my weight, leapt out of the ground with its single long, sinewy root, and I fell over backwards on to the gravel.

On another occasion we had invited a few friends to dinner at our house in Rome. Before the guests arrived my wife, already dressed for the evening and wearing her jewellery, decided to pay a visit to the kitchen to see that all was in order. I followed her. We found the cook in a state of terror over a lobster, an enormous creature with formidable claws and still half alive, which she did not dare to grasp and throw into the pot. Without the slightest fuss my wife went over to the table, picked up the lobster by the back and plunged it into the boiling water. In order to do this, she had, I admit, to keep herself as far away as possible both from the creature and from the cooking-stove. But this prudence on her part only partly explains the ugly, grotesque face that she made and the clearly visible movement of her body, which for a moment looked as though she were trying to execute a provoking shake of the hips beneath the glossy silk of her evening dress.

I imagine that my wife must have gone through these grimaces and contortions countless times and on the most diverse occasions. There remain, however, certain incontestable facts. The contraction of the face and body never happened during love-making. Such contractions, also, were accompanied always by the most profound silence, a silence of suspense which nevertheless seemed more like a repressed cry than a mere calm absence of speech. Finally, the grimace and the contraction of the body seemed always to arise from fright at some unexpected, sudden, lightning-like occurrence. It was a fright, as I have observed, that was closely mingled with sexual attraction.

2

So far, I have spoken of my wife; it is time that I said something of myself. I am tall and thin, with an energetic face and marked, sharp features. Perhaps, on closer examination, certain weaknesses might be discerned in the form of my chin and the shape of my mouth; but the fact remains that I have a strong, determined face which does not at all represent my true character, though it partly explains some contradictions in it. Perhaps my most noteworthy characteristic is lack of depth. Whatever I do or say, the whole of me is contained in what I do or say, and I have nothing in reserve upon which to fall back in the event of my having to retreat. I am, in fact, a man all vanguard, without any main body or rearguard. From this characteristic comes my proneness to enthusiasm: I get excited over any trifle. This enthusiasm of mine, however, is rather like an uncontrolled horse taking a very high fence, having already thrown its rider, who lies biting the dust ten yards behind. What I mean is that it is an enthusiasm that almost always lacks the support of the intimate, effective strength without which any kind of enthusiasm dwindles into mere foolish desire and rhetoric. And I am, in fact, inclined to rhetoric—that is, to the substitution of words for deeds. My rhetoric is of the sentimental kind; I want, for instance, to be in love and often deceive myself into thinking that I *am* in love, when all that I have done is to talk about it—with great feeling, no doubt, but simply to *talk* about it. At such moments tears come easily, I stammer, I assume all the attitudes of over-flowing emotion. But beneath these outward signs of fervour I often conceal a bitter, a positively mean, kind of subtlety which makes me deceitful and does not represent any real strength, being merely the expression of my egoism.

For all those who knew me superficially I was, before I met Leda, what can still be called—but not perhaps for very much longer—a dilettante. A man, that is, who is sufficiently well off to lead a life of leisure, and who devotes that leisure to the understanding and enjoyment of art in its various forms. I suppose that such an assess-ment, anyhow as regards the part that I played in society, was on the whole just. But when I was alone with myself, I was in reality anything but a dilettante: I was a man tormented with anguish and always on the border of despair. There is amongst the works of Poe a story which accurately describes the state of my mind at that time; it is the one in which he relates the adventure of the fisher-man who is drawn with his boat into the coils of a whirl-pool at sea. In his boat he circles all round the walls of the abyss, and with him, above, beside and below him, circle the innumerable remains of former shipwrecks. He knows that as he goes round and round he is approach-ing nearer and nearer to the bottom of the whirlpool where death awaits him, and he knows where all those derelicts come from. Well, my life might have been compared to a perpetual whirlpool. I was held in the swirls of a black vortex, and above me, beneath me, and all round me I saw all the things I loved circling round with me—those things upon which, according to others, I lived, but which I saw overwhelmed with me in the same strange shipwreck. I felt that I was going round in a circle with everything good and beautiful that had ever been created in the world, and I did not cease for one single moment to see the black depth of the vortex that for me and all the other derelicts held the promise of an inevitable end. There were moments when the whirlpool seemed to grow narrower, to flatten out, to go round more slowly and restore me to the calm surface of every-day life; there were also moments when, on the other hand, its circles spun swifter and deeper, and then down I would go, whirling round and round, lower and lower, and down would go, with me, all human art and science. At such times I longed, almost, to be finally swallowed up. In my younger days these crises were frequent, and I can say with truth that there was not a single day between my twentieth and thirtieth years when I did not cherish the idea of suicide. Of course I did not really wish to kill myself (otherwise I should have done so), but this obsession with suicide nevertheless supplied the predominant colour of my mental landscape.

I thought often of possible remedies; and soon I realized that there were only two things that could save me—the love of a woman and artistic creation. It may seem ridiculous for me to mention two things of such importance in so casual a manner, as though it were a matter of a couple of ordinary quack remedies that could be bought at any chemist's shop; but this summary statement merely shows the extreme clarity I had attained, about the age of thirty-five, with regard to the problems of my life. As for love, it seemed to me that I had as much right to it as all other men on this earth; and as for artistic creation, I was convinced that I was led naturally towards it both by my tastes and also by a talent which, in my better moments, I was under the illusion that I possessed.

What happened, on the contrary, was that I never went beyond the first two or three pages of any composition; and with women I never attained to that depth of feeling which convinces both ourselves and others. The thing that did me most harm in both my sentimental and creative efforts was, precisely, that facility of mine for enthusiasm, which was just as prompt to be kindled as it was quick to fade. How many times—in a kiss snatched from unwilling lips, in two or three pages written at furious speed—did I think I had found what I was seeking! And then, with the woman, I would slip at once into a wordy sentimentality that ended by alienating her from me; and, as I wrote, I would lose myself in sophistries, or else in a flood of words into which, for lack of serious inspiration, I was led by a momentary facility. My first impetus was good, and deceived both myself and others; but then some indefinable weakness, cold and discursive, would creep in. And I would realize that in reality I had not loved or written so much as *wished* to love and to write. Sometimes, too, I would find a woman who, either for her own advantage or out of pity, was prepared to allow herself to be taken in and to delude me as well; on other occasions the written page seemed to resist me and to invite me to continue. But I have anyhow one good thing about me—a diffident conscience which halts me in time upon the path of illusion. I would tear up the pages and, under some pretext or other, stop visiting the lady. And so, in such vain attempts, youth fled by.

3

THERE is no need for me to say where and how I first met my wife: it must have been in a drawing-room, or at a watering-place, or somewhere like that. She was about my own age, and it seemed to me that in many respects her life resembled mine. This was true, actually, in only a few respects, and superficial ones at that—merely that she, like me, was well-off and leisured and that she moved in the same circles and led the same kind of life; but to me, with my usual ephemeral enthusiasm, this seemed a most important thing, almost as though I had found my twin soul. She had been married very young, at Milan, her native place, to a man she did not love. The marriage had lasted a couple of years and then the pair had separated and later had obtained a divorce in Switzerland. Since then my wife had always lived alone. The thing that at once aroused in my mind the hope that I had at last found the woman I was looking for, was the confession she made to me the very day that I met her for the first time, to the effect that she was weary of the life she had hitherto led and that she wanted to settle down in an alliance of true affection. In this confession, which was made with great simplicity and without any emotion—just as though it were a question of a practical programme rather than the pathetic aspiration of a loveless life—I seemed to recognize the same state of mind that had dominated me for so many years; and immediately, with my usual initial impulsiveness, I decided that she must be my wife.

I don't think that Leda is very intelligent; but with a mediocre intelligence she nevertheless succeeded, thanks to the importance she assumed in my life and to her air of experience and her nicely calculated mingling of indulgence and irony, in acquiring in my eyes a mysterious authority; owing to which her slightest gesture of understanding and encouragement was, to me, both precious and flattering. I was under the illusion at that time that I had persuaded her to marry me; but I can now say that it was she who had determined upon it and that without that determination on her part the marriage would never have taken place. I was still in the preliminary stages of my courtship, which I imagined would be long and difficult, when she, almost forcing my hand, gave herself to me. But this surrender, which in other women would have seemed to me to be the sign of a facile virtue and would perhaps have made me contemptuous, in her had the same rare and flattering quality as her earlier marks of approbation and encouragement. After I had possessed her, I realized that that mysterious authority of hers remained intact, that it was, in fact, strengthened by the impatience of my senses which had hitherto been unawakened. As, before, she had played upon my need of being understood, so now, with far greater and more instinctive intelligence, she played upon my desire. Thus I discovered that the fleeting, evasive character of her beauty was matched by an analogous character of mind. I was never sure of possessing her completely; and just when I felt I was verging upon satiety, a word, a gesture on her part would, all of a sudden, make me afraid that I was losing her again.

These alternations of possession and despair lasted, one may say, right up till the day of our wedding. By now I was furiously in love with her and I understood that I had, at all costs, to prevent this love coming to an end, like the others that had gone before it, in discouragement and emptiness. Urged on by this fear and at the same time reluctant, and thinking, almost, that I was doing a thing that was altogether too easy, I at last asked her to become my wife, with the certainty of being immediately accepted. Instead of that, I found myself met by an almost astonished refusal, as though in making this proposition I had transgressed some mysterious law of good manners. With this refusal I felt I had reached the darkest depths of my ancient despair. I left her, thinking confusedly that there was nothing left for me and that, if I was not a coward, the time had now really come for me to kill myself. A few days went by and then she telephoned me, asking with surprise why I had not been to see her. I went, and she welcomed me with the sweet but impudent reproof that I had deserted her and had not given her time to reflect. She concluded by saying that, after all, she would agree to become my wife. In two weeks' time we were married.

There began, at once, a period of complete happiness such as I had never known. I loved Leda passionately; yet at the same time I continued to be afraid either that I should stop loving her or that I should stop being loved by her. And so I tried by every possible means to mingle our two lives together. to create bonds between us. As I knew her to be ignorant, I first of all proposed to her a sort of programme of æsthetic education, telling her that she would find just as much pleasure in learning as I should in teaching her. I discovered her, quite unexpectedly, to be extraordinarily docile and sensible. By mutual agreement we arranged a plan and a time-table for our studies, and I undertook to communicate to her, and to make her appreciate, everything that I myself knew and liked. I do not know how far she followed me nor how much she understood: probably very much less than I thought. But, as always, owing to that strange, mysterious authority of hers, I felt I had won a great victory when she said simply: "I like this piece of music . . . this poem is beautiful . . . read me that passage again . . . let's hear that record over again." At the same time, in order to occupy our leisure hours, I was teaching her English. In this she made steady progress, for she had a good memory and a natural inclination. But readings, explanations, lessons were all made attractive and precious in my eyes by her constant kindness and loving affection and goodwill. So that, in a sense, although she was the learner and I the teacher, it was I who felt all the trepidations of the pupil as he progresses slowly through the subjects of his study. And this was right, because the real subject of study between us was love, and every day I seemed to myself to gain a fuller mastery of it.

And indeed, in spite of everything, the surest foundation of our happiness still lay in our love life, which was a thing apart from the tastes that we now shared. I have said already that her beauty, disturbed as it sometimes was by ugly grimaces and contortions, was never unworthy of itself while we were making love. Let me add that the enjoyment of that beauty had now become the central point around which circled the whirlpool of my life, once black and threatening, now luminous, pleasantly slow, regular. How often, as I lay beside her in bed, did I contemplate her naked body and feel almost frightened at seeing it so beautiful, yet at the same time with a beauty which, even under my persevering gaze, defied all definition! How often, as she lay there, flat on her back, her head sunk in the pillow, did I disarrange and rearrange those long, soft, fair tresses of hers, seeking in vain to understand the mysterious feeling of movement which gave them that fluttering, evasive look! How often did I gaze at those enormous blue eyes of hers and wonder where lay the secret of their sweet, troubled expression! How often, after kissing her long and furiously, did I analyse the sensation that my lips still retained, comparing it with the exact shape of *her* lips and hoping to penetrate the significance of that faint smile of almost archaic form which, after the kiss, became visible again at the corners of her big, sinuous mouth—precisely the smile that is to be seen in the earliest Greek statues. I had, in fact, found a mystery as great—or so it seemed to me —as the mysteries of religion: a mystery after my own heart, in which my eyes and my mind, well used to the examination of beauty, could lose themselves at last and find peace, as though in an enchanting, unlimited spaciousness. She appeared to understand all the importance that this kind of adoration acquired for me and allowed herself to be loved with the same untiring docility, the same intelligent complacency with which she allowed herself to be taught.

Perhaps I ought to have been put on my guard, in the

midst of a happiness so complete, by one particular aspect of my wife's attitude, which, anyhow, I think I have already mentioned—her goodwill. In her, clearly, love was not so spontaneous as in me; and there was discernible in her manner towards me an undoubted though mysterious desire to please me, to satisfy me, sometimes even to flatter me—exactly, in fact, what is generally, and not without a trace of contempt, called goodwill. Now it is difficult for goodwill not to conceal something which, if it were by chance revealed, would contradict it and endanger its effects; something that may range from the mere presence of different, hidden pre-occupations to actual duplicity and treachery. But I accepted this goodwill as a proof of her love for me and did not worry, at the time, to investigate what it might conceal, or what the meaning of it might be. I was, in fact, too happy not to be selfish. I knew that for the first time in my life I was in love and, with my usual, rather indiscreet enthusiasm, I attributed to her also the feeling that occupied my own mind.

4

I HAD never spoken to my wife about my literary ambitions because I felt that she would not be able to understand them, and also because I was ashamed to have to confess that they were no more than ambitions, or rather, vain attempts which had never so far been crowned with any success. That year we spent the summer at the seaside, and towards the middle of September we began to discuss our plans for the autumn and winter. I don't know how it came about that I then alluded to my barren efforts; perhaps I may have referred to the long period of idleness into which marriage had led me. "But Silvio, you never told me about it," she exclaimed at once. I answered that I had never spoken of it because, up till that moment, anyhow, I had never succeeded in writing anything that was worth talking about. But she, with her usual affectionate eagerness, merely replied by urging me to show her something I had written. This invitation made me immediately realize that her curiosity flattered me enormously and that, in the long run, her opinion was just as, if not more, important to me than that of a professional man of letters. I knew perfectly well that she was ignorant, that her taste was unreliable, that her approval or her condemnation could have no value; and yet I felt that it now depended upon her whether I continued to write or not. When she insisted, I put up a show of resistance for a short time, and then, having warned her repeatedly that the things I had written were unimportant and that I myself had rejected them, I agreed to read her a brief story that I had written a couple of years before. As I read, it seemed to me that my story was not as bad as I had formerly thought it; and so I went on reading in a firmer and more expressive tone of voice, looking at her every now and then out of the corner of my eye as she sat listening attentively, not showing in any way what effect it was having upon her. When I had finished, I threw the pages aside and exclaimed: "As you see, I was right, it was not worth talking about." And I waited with a strange anxiety for her opinion. She was silent for a moment, as though collecting her impressions, and then she declared, in a decided and peremptory manner, that I was entirely wrong in not attributing any importance to my talent. She said that she liked the story although it had many defects, and she adduced a number of reasons to explain and justify her pleasure. It was not (and how could it have been?) the criticism of an expert; but all the same I felt curiously encouraged. It suddenly seemed to me that her reasons, which were indeed those of an ordinary person with ordinary tastes, might well be worth those of the most refined men of letters; that, after all, there was perhaps in me a tendency to excessive self-criticism, more injurious than useful; and that, in fact, what I had hitherto lacked was not so much talent, perhaps, as affectionate encouragement such as she was at that moment heaping upon me. There is always something false and humiliating in a success amongst one's own family, amongst people whose affection makes them indulgent and partial: a mother, a sister, a wife are always ready to recognize in us the genius that others obstinately deny us, but at the same time their praises do not satisfy us, and we sometimes feel them to be more bitter than frank condemnation. Now I felt nothing of all this with my wife. It seemed to me that she had really liked the story, quite apart from the affection that she bore me. Besides, her praises were discreet and reasoned enough not to seem merely pitying. I asked her, in the end, almost timidly: "Well then, you really think I ought to go on and persevere? . . . Think well over what you say. . . . I've been working for at least ten years without any result. . . . If you tell me to go on, I'll go on . . . but if you tell me to stop, I'll stop and never touch a pen again."

She laughed and said: "You're putting a great responsibility on to me."

I insisted: "Speak as though I were not what I am in relation to you, but a stranger. . . . Say exactly what you think."

"But I've already told you," she replied, "you ought to go on."

"Truly?"

"Yes, truly."

She was silent for a moment and then added: "Now look . . . let's do this. . . . Instead of going back to Rome, let's go and spend a month or two at the villa in Tuscany. . . . You can get down to work there, and I'm sure you'll write something really good."

"But you—you'll be bored."

"Why? *You*'ll be there . . . besides, it'll be a change for me . . . it's so many years since I've led a quiet life."

25

I must admit that it was not so much her reasons and her encouragements that persuaded me as a kind of superstition. I thought that for the first time in my life a kindly star was watching over me, and I said to myself that I ought to assist, in every possible way, this unexpected trend of fortune in my favour. With my wife I had already found the love to which I had aspired in vain for so many years; and perhaps love would now be followed, in its turn, by literary creativeness. I felt, in fact, that I was on the right road; and that the beneficial effects of our meeting were not yet entirely exhausted. I embraced my wife, telling her jokingly that from henceforth she would be my Muse. She did not seem to understand the expression, and asked me again what my decision was.

I answered that, as she had suggested, we would go to the villa in a few days. A week later, in fact, we left the Riviera for Tuscany.

5

THE villa lay in a kind of hollow, at the foot of
some medium-sized mountains, facing a wide,
flat cultivated plain. It was surrounded by a small
park thickly planted with leafy trees; so that there was
no view at all, even from the windows of the top
floor, and one could imagine oneself, not at the edge of
a plain studded with farms and criss-crossed with fields,
but in the depths of a great forest, in a hermit-like
solitude. In the plain, at no great distance from the villa,
lay a big village. The nearest town, on the other hand,
was an hour's cart-ride away, on the top of one of the
hills that rose at the back of the villa. It was a medieval
town, surrounded by battlemented walls, with palaces,
churches, convents, museums; but, as often happens in
Tuscany, it was much poorer than the ugly modern
village that commerce had brought into being in the
plain below.

The villa had been built about a hundred years ago—
judging, at any rate, by the height and size of the trees
in the park. It was a plain, regular building, with three
floors and three windows to each floor. At the front of
the house was an open, gravelled space, shaded by two
horse-chestnut trees; from this space a winding drive led
to the park gate and then, beyond, along the old sur-
rounding wall to the main road. The park, as I have
already said, was small in extent but thickly timbered
and full of shady retreats; its limits were not clearly

27

defined except on one side. On the other sides, without hedges or other dividing lines, the shade of the wood merged into the openness of the cultivated fields. There were a couple of farms attached to the property; and the farm buildings were situated at the edge of the park, on a hill from which one enjoyed a view over the whole of the immense plain. From the villa one could hear, without seeing them, the peasants in the neighbouring fields, urging on their oxen with brief cries; and quite often the farmer's hens would wander all over the park and come pecking right up to the front door.

Inside, the villa was crammed with pieces of old furniture, in which every style of the last century was represented, from "Empire" down to "art nouveau". The last inhabitant, my maternal grandmother, had died there at the age of almost a hundred after having collected, with the avarice and patience of an ant, enough stuff to set up another house of the same size. The rooms contained double the amount of furniture that was needed; and drawers, cupboards and chests were overflowing with a mass of heterogeneous objects—crockery, linen, knick-knacks, rags, old papers, kitchen utensils, lamps, photograph albums and endless other things. The bedrooms were large and dark, with four-post beds, vast chests-of-drawers, dim family portraits. There were, besides, an indefinite number of sitting-rooms, a library with a great many shelves full of old books, most of them volumes on the writings of the Fathers, almanacs, and collections of reviews, and even a small bare room entirely taken up with a billiard-table; but the cloth was torn and there were hardly any cues left and no balls at all. One moved about with difficulty amongst all this creaking old junk, with no free space anywhere; it was as though the real inhabitants of the villa were the pieces of furniture and we merely intruders. However I succeeded in partly clearing the first-floor sitting-room, restoring its original fine Empire appearance; and there I established my own study. We each chose a bedroom; and my wife took as her own sitting-room the drawing-room on the ground floor in which were the only two comfortable armchairs in the house.

We began, from the very first day, to lead a very regular life, almost like that of an industrious monastery. In the morning the old servant carried the tray into my wife's room and we had breakfast together, she in bed and I sitting beside her. Then I left her, went into my study, sat down at the desk and worked, or at least tried to work, until midday. In the meantime my wife, after lying in bed for a little, would get up, make a lengthy and meticulous toilet and, while she was dressing, give the cook her orders for the day. About midday I would rise from my work and go downstairs, where my wife would be waiting for me. We took our meals in a small dining-room, in front of a french window giving on to the park. After lunch we drank our coffee outside, in the shade of the chestnut tree. Then we would go up to our rooms for a short rest. We met again at tea in the drawing-room on the ground floor. There was not a great variety of walks; Tuscany, where it is cultivated, is more like a garden, though without seats or paths, than open country: so we went either along the winding tracks that led across the fields from one farm to another; or we walked along the grassy bank of a canal that crossed the whole length of the plain; or, again, we strolled along the main road, but without ever going as far as either the village or the town. When we returned from our walk, which never lasted more than an hour, I gave my wife her English lesson and then, if there was still time, I read aloud to her or made her read to me. Then we dined, and after dinner we read again or conversed. Finally we went, not very late, to our rooms, or rather I followed my wife into hers. This was our moment for making love—towards which, in truth, our whole day had been tending. I found my wife always ready and always docile, as though she were conscious of providing both herself and me with a reward and an outlet after so many hours of tranquillity. In the rustic night that looked in through the wide-open windows, its deep silence broken only at rare intervals by the cry of a bird, in that dim and lofty room, our love would burst into sudden flame and burn long and silently, clear and living like the flame of the old oil lamps that once had illumined those sombre apartments. I felt that I loved my wife more each day, the feeling of each evening nourishing itself and gathering strength from that of the evening before; and she, on her side, seemed never to exhaust the treasure of her affectionate, sensual compliance. During those nights, for the first and, perhaps, the last time in my life, I seemed to grasp the meaning of what true conjugal passion can be—that mixture of violent devotion and lawful sensuality, of exclusive, limitless possession and confident joy in that possession. For the first time I understood the sometimes indiscreet sense of ownership that some men attach to the marriage relationship, saying "my wife" in the same way that they say "my house" or "my dog" or "my motor car."

The thing which, on the other hand, did not go too well, though conditions were so favourable, was my work. My idea was to write a long story or short novel, and the subject, the story of a marriage, interested me passionately. It was *our* story, the story of my wife and me, and I felt that I had the whole thing already fixed in my mind, separated into single, distinct episodes, so that it could be filled out with the greatest ease. But when I sat myself down in front of my paper and started trying to write, the thing would get all tangled up. Either the sheet would be filled with words and phrases crossed out, or I would go straight ahead for a page or two and then realize that I had been piling up a mass of vague generalizations and sentences without concrete meaning; or again, after writing the first few lines, I would stop and remain motionless and absorbed in front of the blank page, looking as if I were in the act of reflecting deeply, but, in reality, with an empty head and a mind that had ceased to function. I have a highly developed critical sense, and for some years I wrote criticisms for newspapers and reviews; and I very soon realized, therefore, that my work was not merely not progressing but was actually going worse than it had before. Formerly I had been capable of fixing my mind on a subject and developing it, so to speak, in an orderly manner, without, it is true, ever attaining to poetry, but always keeping up a certain standard of elegance and clarity in my writing. Now, on the other hand, I saw that it was not only the subject-matter, but also my former control of style, that was eluding me. In spite of myself, some malign force would cram my page with repetitions, solecisms, obscure, limping sentences, vague adjectives, over-emphatic idioms, commonplaces, hackneyed phrases. But above all I was clearly conscious that what I lacked was rhythm—I mean that regular, harmonious breath that sustains the process of development in prose, as metre sustains and regulates that of poetry. I remembered that once upon a time I had possessed this rhythm—in a very measured and modest, but still sufficient, degree. But that too had now deserted me: I stumbled and stammered and lost myself in a ferment of discord and clamour.

Perhaps I should have let my work go altogether, since the love I felt for my wife sufficed for my happiness, if it had not been that she herself urged me to persevere. Not a day passed that she did not ask me, with an affectionate and at the same time exacting solicitude, how my work was going; and I, ashamed of confessing that it was not going at all, answered her rather vaguely that it was progressing steadily. She seemed to attach the greatest importance to this work, as though it were something for which she herself was responsible; and I felt more strongly every day that I now owed it not so much to myself as to her to accomplish the writing of my story. It was a proof of love that I had to furnish for her, as a demonstration of the profound change that her presence had wrought in my life. That was what I had meant when I had embraced her and whispered that henceforth she would be my Muse. With that daily enquiry of hers about the employment of my morning she had, without knowing it, ended by making it a point of honour with me—rather like the mythological ladies who ask the knight to slay the monster and bring back the golden fleece; and never has the fable been known in which a cowed and contrite knight has returned empty-handed, confessing that he had been unable to find the fleece and that he had not had the courage to face the dragon. This point of honour took on an even more urgent and peremptory aspect owing to the particular character of her insistence, which was not that of a cultivated woman versed in the problems of intellectual labour but that of an ignorant and ingenuous mistress who probably imagined that writing poetry was, after all, a simple matter of will and application. Once, during our daily walk, I tried to draw her attention to the many difficulties and the not infrequent impossibilities in literary creation; but I saw at once that she could not understand me. "I'm not a writer," she said, after listening to what I had to say, "nor have I any literary ambitions . . . but, if I had, I think I should have lots of things to say . . . and, in the conditions for working that you have here, I'm sure I should be able to say them very well." She looked at me sideways for a moment and then added, with grave coquettishness: "Remember you promised to write a story with me in it . . . and now you must keep your promise." I said nothing, but I could not help thinking angrily of the many pages bristling with cancellations and superimposed lines piling up on my desk.

I had noticed that in the morning, after passing the night, or part of the night, with my wife, when I sat

33

down to work I felt an almost uncontrollable inclination to let my mind wander and do nothing; my head felt empty, I had an odd sensation of lightness at the back of my neck and a sort of lack of solidity in my limbs. Our moral relationship with ourselves is sometimes extremely obscure; not so the physical relationship, which, particularly at a mature age, if a man is well-balanced and healthy, reveals itself with perfect clarity. It did not take me much time or thought to conclude, rightly or wrongly, that this inability to work, this impossibility of keeping my mind on the subject, this temptation to idleness, must be attributed to the physical emptying of myself that occurred always after making love the previous night. Sometimes I would rise from my desk and look at myself in the mirror: in the tired, relaxed muscles of my face, in the shadows under my eyes and their lustreless expression, in the languid slackness of my whole attitude I could recognize precisely the lack of that vigour of which, on the other hand, I was conscious in myself every night, at the moment when I lay down and took my wife in my arms. I realized that I did not attack my paper because, the evening before, I had exhausted all my aggressive force in my wife's embrace; I knew that what I was giving to my wife I was taking away, in equal measure, from my work. This was not a precise thought—not as precise, anyhow, as it now appears when I express it; rather it was a diffused sensation, a persistent suspicion, almost the beginning of an obsession. My creative force, I felt, was drained out of me every night from the middle of my body; and next day there was not enough left to rise upwards and fortify my brain. The obsession, as can be seen, took shape in images, in comparisons, in concrete metaphors which gave me a physical, almost a scientific, sense of my own importance.

Obsessions either close up like abscesses which can find no outlet and slowly mature until their final, terrible outburst, or else, in more healthy persons, they find, sooner or later, some adequate means of elimination. I went on for several more days making love to my wife at night and spending the day thinking that it was just because I had made love to her that I could not work. At this point I ought to say that this obsession made no change whatever, not merely in my affection for my wife, but even in the actual physical transport: at the moment of love I forgot my scruples and almost deceived myself, in the temporary arrogance of desire, into thinking that I was strong enough to carry through both love-making and work. But next day the obsession would return; and at night I found myself seeking love again if only to console myself for having been defeated in my work and in order, at the same time, to rediscover the fleeting illusion of inexhaustible vigour. At last, after spinning round for some time in this vicious circle, I decided, one evening, to speak. I was encouraged to do this also by the idea that it was she, after all, who urged me to work, and that, if it was really of importance to her, as it seemed to be, that I should write the story, she would understand and accept my reasons. When we were lying side by side on the bed, I began: "Listen, I must tell you a thing that I've never told you before."

It was hot, and we were both lying naked on top of

the bedclothes, she on her back, with her hands clasped at the back of her neck and her head on the pillow, and I at her side. Scarcely moving her lips, and looking at me in her usual troubled, elusive way, she said: "Tell me."

"It's this," I went on. "You want me to write this story?"

"Certainly I do."

"This story which tells about you and me?"

"Yes."

"With things as they are now, I shall never succeed in writing it."

"What d'you mean, things as they are now?"

I hesitated a moment, and then I said: "We make love every evening, don't we? Well, I feel that all the force that I need for writing this story is taken away from me when I'm with you. If it goes on like this, I shall never be able to write it."

She looked at me with those huge blue eyes of hers, which were dilated, one would have said, by the effort of understanding me. "But how do other writers manage?" she asked.

"I don't know how they manage. . . . But I imagine that they lead chaste lives, at any rate while they're working."

"But D'Annunzio," she said, "I've heard that he had such a number of mistresses . . . how did he manage?"

"I don't know," I answered, "whether he had such a great number of mistresses. What he had was a few celebrated mistresses, about whom everybody talked, he himself most of all . . . but in my opinion, he arranged

36

his life very well. . . . Now Baudelaire's chastity, for instance, is well known."

She said nothing. I felt that all my reasoning came painfully close to the ridiculous, but I had begun now and I had to go on. I resumed, in a gentle, caressing tone of voice: "Look, I'm not really set on writing this story nor, in general, on becoming a writer. I'll give it up with the greatest ease. . . . The important thing, for me, is our love."

She answered at once, with a frown: "But I want you to write it. I want you to become a writer."

"Why?"

"Because you're a writer already," she said rather confusedly and almost with irritation. "I feel that you've got a great deal to say. . . . Besides, you ought to work, like everyone else. You can't just lead an idle life and be content merely with making love to me. You've got to become somebody." She stumbled over her words, and it was clear that she did not know how to express that stubborn desire of hers to see me do what she wanted me to do.

"There's no need for me to become a writer," I answered, though this time I felt I was telling anyhow a partial lie; "I can perfectly well not do anything . . . or rather, I can go on doing what I've done hitherto—read, appreciate, understand, admire the works of others . . . and love you. Or again, so as not to be idle, as you say, I could perhaps take up some other profession, some other occupation. . . ."

"No, no, no," she said hastily, shaking not only her head but her body too, as though she wanted to express

37

this refusal with her whole self, "you've got to write—you've got to become a writer."

After these words we remained silent for a moment. Then she said: "If what you say is true . . . then we must change everything."

"What d'you mean?"

"We mustn't make love any more until you've finished your story. . . . Then, when you've finished, we'll begin again."

I must confess that I was immediately tempted to accept this strange and slightly ridiculous proposal. My obsession was still strong and it made me forget how much selfishness, and therefore falseness, had been at the root of it. But I repressed this first impulse and, embracing her, said: "You love me and this proposal of yours is the greatest proof of your love that you could give me. . . . But the fact that you've made it is enough for me. Let's go on loving each other and not think about anything else."

"No, no," she said imperiously, pushing me away, "that's what we must do—now that you've told me."

"Are you offended?"

"Really, Silvio, why should I be offended? I truly want you to write that story, that's all. . . . Don't be silly." And as she said this, as if to underline the affectionate quality of her insistence, she put her arms round me.

We went on like this for a little, I defending myself and she insisting, imperious, inflexible. Finally I said: "All right, I'll try . . . it may be that all this isn't true and that I'm simply a person without any literary talent."

"That isn't true, Silvio, and you know it."

"All right then," I concluded with an effort, "as you like. . . . But remember it was you who wished it."

"Of course."

We were silent again for some little time, then I made a movement as if to take her in my arms. But she at once pushed me away: "No," she said, "from this evening onwards we must stop doing that." She laughed and, as if to soften the bitterness of her refusal, took my face between her long, slim hands—delicately, as one takes hold of a precious vase—and said: "Now you'll see you'll write all sorts of fine things—I'm sure of it." She looked closely at me, and then added in a strange way: "D'you love me?"

"You don't need to ask me that," I said, deeply moved.

"Well, you shall have me again only when you've read me the story. . . . Remember that."

"And supposing I'm not able to write it?"

"You've got to be able."

She was imperious; and this imperiousness of hers, ingenuous, inexperienced, but at the same time inflexible, was strangely pleasing to me. I thought again of the knight in the legend whose lady, in exchange for her love, demands that he shall kill the dragon and bring back the fleece; but this time I thought of him without anger, almost with admiration. She knew nothing of poetry, just as the lady probably knew nothing of the fleece and the dragon; but just because of this her command pleased me. It was as though it were a confirmation of the miraculous, heaven-sent character of all creative work. All at once there came to me a sudden exaltation mingled with confidence and hope and gratitude. I put my face

39

close to hers, kissed her tenderly and whispered: "For love of you I will become a writer . . . not on my own merit, but for love of you." She said nothing. I got down from the bed and slipped out of the room.

After that I took up my work again with renewed courage; and I soon realized that my calculations had not been wrong and that, somehow or other, even if there was not that connection between love and work that I had tried to perceive, the obsession of impotence that had oppressed me hitherto could never have been dispelled except in the way I had chosen. Every morning I felt myself stronger, more aggressive as I faced my paper, more—at least, so it seemed to me—creative. And so, after love, the greatest aspiration of my life was fulfilled: poetry, too, smiled upon me. Every morning I wrote from ten to twelve pages, my pen flowing rapidly and impetuously but in no disorderly or uncontrolled fashion; and then, for the rest of the day, I was left dazed, stunned, half alive, with the feeling that, outside my work, nothing now mattered in my life, not even my love for my wife. All that remained after those ardent morning hours was the residue, the ashes and cinders of a glorious blaze; and until the new blaze was kindled, next morning, I was left strangely inert and detached, filled with an almost morbid sense of well-being, indifferent to everything. I saw that, if this rhythm continued, I should soon have finished my work, perhaps even earlier than I had foreseen; and I felt that I must exert myself in every possible way to gather in the last grain of this bountiful and unexpected harvest: nothing else, for the moment, mattered. To say that I was happy would be saying too little, and at the same time too much: I was, for the first time in my life, outside myself, in an independent, perfect world all made up of harmony and certainty. This state made me selfish; and I suppose that, if my wife had fallen ill at that moment, I should have felt no other anxiety but that of a possible interruption of my work. Not that I did not love my wife; as I have said, I loved her more than ever: but she was, as it were, relegated to a detached, remote region, together with all the other things that had nothing to do with my work. I was, in fact, convinced, for the first time in my life, not merely that I had found self-expression—a thing that I had attempted a thousand times without success— but also that my self-expression was taking a perfect and complete form. In other words, I had the precise sensation, founded, it seemed to me, on my experience as a man of letters, that I was writing a masterpiece.

6

AFTER working all the morning, I spent the afternoon in the usual way, being careful only to avoid sudden emotions and shocks and distractions; though in appearance far removed from literature, I was in reality, in the dark depths of my mind, gloating with affectionate delight over what I had written during the morning and what I intended to write next day. Later, at bed-time, I said good-night to my wife on the landing between the doors of our two rooms, and went straight to bed. I slept with a feeling of confidence I had never known, conscious, as it were, that I was accumulating the fresh energies that I would expend upon my work next morning. On awaking I felt ready and well-disposed, light and vigorous, my head filled with ideas which had sprung up there during sleep like grass in a meadow during a night of rain. I sat down at my desk, hesitated only one minute, and then my pen, as if moved by an independent will, would start running over the sheets of paper, from one word to another, from one line to the next, as though between my mind and the ceaselessly unfolding arabesque of ink upon paper there were neither interruptions of continuity nor any difference in material. I had inside my head a large and inexhaustible reel of thread and, by my act of writing, all I did was to pull and unwind this thread, arranging it on the sheets of paper in the elegant black patterns of handwriting; and in this reel of thread there were no knots or gaps; and it went round and round in my head as I unwound it; and I had the feeling that, the more I unwound it, the more there was to unwind. As I have already said, I would write from ten to twelve pages, urging myself to the point of physical exhaustion, fearful above all that this flood of activity might, for some mysterious reason, suddenly decrease or even dry up altogether. At last, when I could do no more, I would rise from my desk with tottering legs and a feeling of giddiness in my head, walk over to a mirror and look at myself. There in the mirror I could see, not one but two, or even three, images of myself slowly doubling and redoubling as they mingled and criss-crossed each other. A long and careful toilet would put me right again, although, as I have said, I remained dazed and stunned all the rest of the day.

Later, at table, I ate with a hearty, automatic appetite, feeling, almost, that I was not a human being at all but an empty machine that required to be filled up again with fuel after several hours of fierce efficiency. As I ate I laughed and joked and even made puns—quite a new thing for me, who am usually serious and thoughtful. As always happens with me when, for some reason or other, I yield to enthusiasm, there was a sort of indiscreet quality, almost an immodesty, in this exuberance of mine: I was aware of it, but whereas once I should have been ashamed of myself for giving way to it, I was now almost pleased with myself for displaying it. There I was, sitting at table, facing my wife, in the act of eating; but really I was not there at all. The best part of me had remained in my study upstairs, at the writing table, pen in hand. The rest of the day passed in the same atmosphere of gaiety—the rather disconnected, extravagant gaiety of a drunkard.

Had I been less enthusiastic, less intoxicated with good fortune, I might perhaps have recognized in the productiveness of those days the presence of that same quality of goodwill that I sometimes thought I could detect in my wife's attitude towards me. To express it differently, and without inferring that the story I was in process of writing was not the masterpiece I believed it to be, the thought might have entered my head that all this was too good to be true. Perfection is not a human thing; and more often than not, it resides in falsehood rather than in truth, whether that falsehood becomes established in the relations between us and other people or presides over the relations between us and ourselves. For, in order to avoid the ugly irregularities and roughnesses of the truth, a fabrication which achieves its purpose without obstacles or misgivings is more effective than a scrupulous mode of action which sticks closely to the matter in hand. As I have said, I might have become suspicious of my affairs going so smoothly, after ten or more years of fruitless attempts. But happiness, besides making us selfish, often makes us thoughtless and superficial as well. I told myself that my meeting with my wife had been the spark which had at last set alight this great and generous blaze; and beyond the recognition of this fact I did not go.

I was so much absorbed in my work that I did not pay much attention to a small but curious incident that took place at that time. I have a very sensitive skin and shaving is always a difficulty to me—that is, it is always inclined to produce a rash or other irritations. For this reason I have never been able to shave myself and have always made use, as I still do, of the services of a barber. Even at the villa, as everywhere else, I arranged to be shaved by a barber every morning. He came from the village nearby, where he kept the only barber's shop, which was, in truth, a very modest one. He used to come on a bicycle and made his appearance exactly at half-past twelve, having in fact closed his shop at twelve. His arrival was the signal for me to stop work. It coincided likewise with the best moment of my day, with the release of that indiscreet and entirely physical gaiety I have already described, which came from a sense of work well done.

This barber was a short, broad-shouldered man, completely bald from front to back, with a thick neck and a plump face. In figure he was thickset but not fat. In his face, which was of a uniform yellowish brown so that he looked as though he still had the remains of an attack of jaundice, the most noticeable feature was the eyes, large and round with very conspicuous whites, and with a clear, questioning, surprised, possibly ironical look in them. He had a small nose and a wide but lipless mouth, in which his rare smiles disclosed two rows of dark and broken teeth. His chin retreated sharply, and in it was a strange, repellent dimple, like a navel. Antonio's voice—for that was his name—was soft and extraordinarily quiet; and his hand, as I noticed from the very first day, had an uncommon lightness and dexterity. He was a man of about forty and, as I knew, had a wife and five

45

children. One last detail: he was not a Tuscan but a Sicilian, from a village in the middle of Sicily. As the result of an amorous connection which he had formed during his military service, he had been induced to marry and settle down in this village, where he had subsequently opened a barber's shop. His wife worked on a farm, but she left it on Saturdays and went and helped her husband to shave the numerous clients who flocked to the shop on the day before the holiday.

Antonio was very punctual. Every day at half-past twelve I could hear, through the open window, the crunching of the gravel beneath his bicycle wheels in the drive below; and this, for me, was the signal for breaking off work. A moment later he would be knocking at the door of my study; and I, rising from my desk, would shout joyfully to him to come in. He would open the door, enter, close it again carefully and, with a slight bow, wish me good-morning. With him came the maid, carrying a small jug of boiling water which she would put down on a little wheeled table where soap, brush and razors were laid out. Antonio would push this little table close to the armchair in which I, in the meantime, had seated myself. He would spend some time stropping the razor, with his back turned to me; then, having poured some of the hot water into a small basin he would wet the brush and stir it round and round for a long time in the soap-bowl. Finally, holding up the foamy brush in the air like a torch, he would turn towards me. The process of soaping me was interminable; he never left off until the whole of the lower part of my face was enveloped in an enormous mass of white froth. Only then did he put down the brush and take up the razor.

I have described these perfectly ordinary actions in minute detail so as to give a feeling of the slowness and precision of his movements—and at the same time to convey an idea of the readiness of my own mind to endure, in fact to enjoy, that slowness and that precision. Usually I do not enjoy being shaved, and the stupid fussiness of some barbers irritates me. But with Antonio it was different. I felt that the only time that had any value was the time that I spent at my desk, before his arrival. Afterwards, whether the time was devoted to shaving, or to reading, or to conversation with my wife, it was all the same to me. It was all time that did not count, from the moment that it had nothing to do with my work; and how I employed it was a matter of indifference to me.

Antonio was taciturn; I, on the other hand, was not, for, after the restraint and the effort of my work, I felt an irresistible need for some sort of outlet for my happiness. And so I talked to him about anything that came into my head, about life in the village, about its inhabitants, about the harvest and his family and the local gentry and things like that. One subject that interested me more than others was, I remember, the contrast between the barber's birthplace in the south and his country of adoption. Nothing could be more different from Sicily than Tuscany. And indeed, more than once, I succeeded in drawing curious remarks from him about Tuscany and the Tuscans in which I thought I could detect a tinge of contempt and disgust. But for the most part Antonio would answer with extreme sobriety; yet, as I noticed, with remarkable exactness. He had a way of speaking that was terse, reticent, sententious, perhaps ironical, but with an irony so slight as to be intangible. Sometimes, if I was roaring with laughter at one of my own jokes or if I became heated as I was speaking, he would stop soaping my face or shaving me and, holding the brush or the razor in mid-air, would wait patiently until I was silent and calm again.

7

IN talking to him, I had no definite purpose in mind, as I think I have already made clear; yet, after some time, I realized that, in spite of all the confidences I had forced from him, I had never penetrated the centre of his mind nor fathomed its chief preoccupation. Although he was poor and had a large family, he did not seem to worry much about money. He spoke of his family with detachment, without either affection or severity or any other particular feeling, as one speaks of something inevitable and perfectly natural. In politics, as I at once saw, he took no interest at all. His trade, although he knew it thoroughly and liked his work, did not appear to mean anything more to him than the mere means of earning a living. In the end I said to myself that there was something mysterious about him; but not more so than in the case of many people of the working class, to whom wealthier people like to attribute thoughts and cares that match their position and then find that they are engrossed by the same things that matter to everybody.

While Antonio was shaving me, my wife would usually come into the room and sit in the sun in the open window, with her manicure-case or else a book. I do not know why, but this morning visit of my wife's while Antonio was shaving me gave me great pleasure. Like Antonio, she was a mirror in which I gazed at the reflection of my own happiness. Like Antonio, though in a different manner, by coming in and sitting down in the room where I had just been working, she helped to carry me back into the atmosphere of everyday life—I mean that indulgent, calm, ordered atmosphere which permitted me to go forward with my work in security and tranquillity. Every now and then I would interrupt my chatter with the barber and ask her how she was or what book she was reading or what she was doing. She would answer quietly, soberly, without raising her eyes and without breaking off her reading or the filing of her nails. The sun shone on her fair hair falling loose in two long waves on either side of her face; behind her bent head I could see, through the wide-open window, no less luminous, the trees in the garden and the blue sky. This same sunshine awakened tawny reflections in the furniture, darted blinding rays from Antonio's razor, and spread benignly from the window-sill to the most distant corners of the room, bringing to life the faded colours and dusty surfaces of the worn stuffs and the old tables and chairs. I was so happy that I thought, on one of those mornings: "As long as I live, I shall remember this scene . . . myself lying back in the armchair, with Antonio shaving me . . . the window open, the room filled with sunshine and my wife sitting over there, in the sun."

One day my wife came in in a dressing-gown and told Antonio that she wanted him to dress her hair for her. All that was needed, she said, was a touch with the curling-iron; she had already washed it herself, that morning. She asked Antonio whether he knew how to wave hair, and when he said yes, she requested him, after he had finished with me, to go to her room. When my

wife had gone out, I asked Antonio if he had ever been
a ladies' hairdresser and he replied, not without vanity,
that all the girls of the countryside came to him to have
their hair done. I was surprised, and he confirmed that
nowadays even the most rustic peasant-girls wanted
permanent waves. "They're more particular than town
ladies," he concluded with a smile; "they're never
satisfied . . . sometimes they're enough to drive you
mad." He shaved me with his usual slowness and precision. Then, after putting the razors all in order, he left
me and went to my wife's room.

After Antonio had gone, I sat down in the sun in the
armchair in which my wife generally sat, a book in my
hand. I remember that it was Tasso's *Aminta*, which I
had started to re-read at that time. I was conscious of
being in a particularly lucid and sensitive state of mind
and the charm of that graceful poem, which accorded so
well with the luminous, gentle quality of the day, soon
made me forget that I was waiting. Now and then, at a
more than usually melodious line, I would raise my eyes
to the window, repeating it in my mind; and each time
I made this movement I seemed to become conscious of
my happiness, like someone who moves about in a well-
warmed bed and is conscious, each time he moves, of
its comfort. Antonio's job with my wife took about
three-quarters of an hour. Finally I heard him go out on
to the drive, say goodbye to the maid in a quiet voice,
and then I heard the crunch of the gravel under his
bicycle wheels as he went further and further away.
A few minutes later my wife came into the room.

I rose to my feet in order to look at her. Antonio, so

it seemed, had solved the problem by covering her whole head with curls and transforming the smooth, loose arrangement of her hair into a sort of eighteenth-century wig. All those curls piled one on top of another and sprouting out round her long, thin face gave her, at first sight, an odd appearance, like a smartly dressed peasant-woman. This look of rusticity was enhanced by a little bunch of fresh flowers—I think they were red geraniums —pinned on just above her left temple.

"Splendid!" I cried, with a burst of gaiety. "Antonio's certainly a wizard. . . . Mario and Attilio in Rome can go and bury their heads, they're not worthy even to tie his shoes. . . . You look just like one of the little peasant-girls from round about here when they go to the fair on Sunday . . . and those flowers are really marvellous. . . . Let's look at you." As I said this I tried to make her turn slowly round, so as better to admire the barber's achievement.

But, to my surprise, my wife's face was clouded by an ill-humour that I could not account for. Her big lower lip was trembling—always a sign of anger, with her. Finally, with a movement of intense disgust, she pushed me away, saying: "Please don't make jokes. . . . I'm not at all in the mood for joking."

I did not understand, and I went on: "Come on, you don't need to be ashamed. I assure you, Antonio's done an excellent job . . . you look splendid. . . . Don't worry, you'll cut a good figure at the fair next Sunday—and if you go to the dance, you'll certainly have several pro-posals of marriage!"

As can be seen, I imagined that her ill-humour was due

to what Antonio had done: I knew her to be extremely vain and it would not have been the first time that an unskilful hairdresser had aroused her anger. But she thrust me away again, this time with a look of resentment, and repeated: "I've already asked you not to make jokes."

It suddenly dawned upon me that her displeasure was caused by something other than her *coiffure*. "But why?" I asked. "What has happened?"

She had walked over to the window and was looking out, her two hands on the sill.

Suddenly she turned. "What has happened is that tomorrow you must kindly do me the favour of changing your barber. I don't want that Antonio here any more."

I was astonished. "But why? He's not a town barber, I know that of course . . . but he does all right for me. . . . *You* don't have to make use of him again."

"Oh, Silvio," she burst forth in anger, "why won't you understand me? It's not a question of whether he's good at his job—what does that matter?"

"But what's it all about, then?"

"He was disrespectful to me . . . and I don't want to see him any more—ever again."

"He was disrespectful to you? What d'you mean?"

There must have been in my expression and the tone of my voice still something of the thoughtless indifference that possessed me every morning at that time, for she added scornfully: "But what does it matter to you if Antonio is disrespectful to me? Of course, it means nothing to you."

I was afraid I had offended her; going up to her, I said,

53

seriously: "Forgive me . . . perhaps I hadn't quite understood. But do please tell me in what way he was lacking in respect."

"I tell you, he was disrespectful," she cried with sudden rage, turning towards me a second time, with nostrils quivering and an expression of hardness in her eyes; "that's quite enough. . . . He's a horrible man—send him away, get someone else. . . . I don't want him about the place any more."

"I don't understand," I said; "he's a man who's usually most respectful—serious, in fact. . . . A family man. . . ."

"Yes," she repeated, with a sarcastic shrug of the shoulders, "a family man."

"But now will you please tell me what he did to you?"

We went on disputing like this for a while, I insisting on knowing in what way Antonio had shown lack of respect, and she refusing to provide any explanation but merely repeating her accusation. In the end, after a great deal of furious wrangling, I thought I understood what had happened. In order to dress her hair, it had been necessary for Antonio to stand very close to the armchair in which she was sitting. It had appeared to her that more than once he had tried to brush against her shoulder and her arm with his body. I say it *appeared* to her; for she herself admitted that the barber had continued his work imperturbably, remaining all the time silent and respectful. But these contacts, she swore, were not fortuitous; she had observed that they had an intention, a purpose behind them. She was sure that Antonio had intended, by means of these contacts, to establish a relationship with her, to make her an improper proposal.

54

"But are you quite sure?" I asked at last, astonished.

"How could I *not* be sure? Oh, Silvio, how can you doubt what I say?"

"But it might have been just an impression."

"Impression?—nonsense. . . . Besides, it's enough just to look at him. He's sinister, that man . . . completely bald, and with that neck and those eyes that always look up at you from under his eyelids and never straight in the face. . . . That man's baldness is outrageous. . . . Don't you see what I mean? Are you blind?"

"It might have been an accident. . . . A barber's work forces him to come very close to his client."

"No, it wasn't an accident. . . . *Once* might perhaps have been an accident, but several times, all the time—no, it wasn't an accident."

"Let's see," I said; and I cannot deny that I felt some amusement in carrying out this species of inquest: "you sit down on this chair. . . . I'll be Antonio. Now let's see."

She was boiling over with impatience and anger; but she obeyed, though with a bad grace, and sat down on the chair. I took up a pencil, pretending it was the curling-iron, and leant over as though to curl her hair. And in fact, in that position, just as I had imagined, the lower part of my stomach was exactly at the level of her arm and shoulder and I could not help brushing against her.

"Look," I said, "it's just as I thought. . . . He couldn't help touching you. If anything, then, it was you who ought to have drawn away a little to the other side."

"That's just what I did; but then he went round to the other side."

55

"Perhaps he had to do that in order to do your hair on that side."

"But, Silvio—is it possible you can be so blind, so stupid? One would say you were doing it on purpose. . . . I tell you, there was a deliberate intention in those contacts."

A question was on my lips, but I hesitated to ask it. Finally I said: "There's contact and contact. . . . Did it seem to you that while he was touching you he was—how shall I say?—excited?"

She was sitting huddled in the armchair, a finger between her teeth, with an expression of strange perplexity on her still angry face. "Certainly," she answered, shrugging her shoulders.

I was afraid I had not understood properly, or had not made myself clear. "In fact," I insisted, "it was obvious that he was excited?"

"Well, yes."

I now realized that I was perhaps even more astonished by my wife's behaviour than by Antonio's. She was no longer a girl, but a woman of considerable experience; besides, I was not ignorant that, with regard to things of this kind, she had always had a sort of gay cynicism. All that I knew of her led me to think that she would not have made any fuss over this incident; or, at most, that she would have told me about it in a detached, ironical way. Instead of which, all this rage and hatred! I said, perplexed: "But look, all this still doesn't mean anything. . . . It might happen to anybody to get excited by certain contacts without wanting to, in fact not wanting to at all. . . . It's happened to me sometimes in a crowd or in a tram, that I found myself wedged against some woman and got excited without meaning to. . . . The spirit is willing," I added jokingly, intending to calm her down, "but the flesh is weak. . . . Why, good heavens . . ."

She said nothing. She appeared to be thinking deeply, biting the tip of her finger and looking towards the window. I thought she had calmed down and I went on, still in a joking manner: "Even saints have their temptations, so what about barbers! . . . Poor Antonio, when he least expected it, made the unwilling discovery that you're a very beautiful and very desirable woman. Being close to you, he wasn't able to control himself . . . probably it was just as disagreeable for him as for you—and that's all there is to it."

She was still silent. I concluded, cheerfully: "When all's said and done I think you ought to make light of this incident. It wasn't so much lack of respect as a kind of homage—a bit coarse and countrified, I agree, but— well, fashions vary, you know."

Carried away by the usual bold gaiety that came over me after my work, I was becoming, as can be seen, deplorably facetious. I realized this just in time and, forcing myself to be serious again, I added hastily: "Forgive me, I know I'm being vulgar—but to tell you the truth I cannot manage to take this whole business seriously . . . all the more so because I'm sure Antonio is innocent."

She spoke at last. "None of this interests me," she said; "what I want to know is whether you're prepared to send him away—that's all."

I have already observed that happiness makes us

57

selfish. At that moment, probably, my selfishness reached its highest point. For I knew that there was no other barber in the village. I knew, besides, that it would be impossible to find one in the town who would be ready to travel several miles every day in order to come and shave me. It would mean giving up the idea of a barber altogether and shaving myself. But, since I don't really know how to shave myself, it would have led to skin inflammations, scratches, cuts and, in fact, all sorts of unpleasantnesses. Instead of which, I wanted everything to go on undisturbed and unchanged as long as I was working, I wanted nothing to come and upset the state of profound quietness which, rightly or wrongly, I considered to be absolutely indispensable if my work were to go well. I forced myself, all at once, to be very serious and said: "But, my dear, you haven't succeeded in convincing me that Antonio was really lacking in respect towards you—I mean intentionally. . . . Why should I sack him? For what reason? What excuse could I make?"

"Any excuse. . . . Tell him we're leaving."

"It isn't true . . . and he would find out at once."

"What does that matter to me?—provided I don't see him again."

"But it's not possible. . . ."

"You won't even do this to oblige me," she cried, exasperated.

"But, my dear, think for a moment. . . . Why should I give gratuitous offence to a poor man who . . .?"

"Poor man, indeed! He's an outrageous, horrible, sinister man."

"Besides, what am I to do about shaving? You know perfectly well that there are no barbers within fifteen miles of this house."

"Shave yourself, then."

"But I can't shave myself."

"What sort of a man are you, if you can't even shave yourself?"

"No, I *can't* shave myself—so what am I to do?"

"Grow a beard, then."

"Please, for goodness' sake! I shouldn't be able to sleep a wink."

She was silent for a time, and then, in a voice in which there seemed to be an echo of despair, she cried: "Well then, you refuse to do what I ask you—you refuse to do it."

"But, Leda . . ."

"Yes, you refuse to do it . . . and you want to force me to see that horrible, disgusting man again . . . you want to force me to come in contact with him."

"But I don't want to force you to do anything. You needn't appear. . . . You can stay in your own room. . . ."

"So I've got to hide myself in my own house, because you won't do this to oblige me."

"But, Leda . . ."

"Leave me alone." I had moved close beside her, and I was trying to take her hand. "Leave me alone. . . . I want you to send him away, d'you understand?"

I decided that I must at last take up an attitude of firmness. "Listen, Leda," I said, "please don't go on like this. This is just an idle caprice and I don't intend to yield to caprices. . . . Now I shall try and find out whether what you state is true; but only if the truth of your accusations can be proved shall I dismiss this man—not otherwise."

She looked at me for some time and then, without saying a word, got up and left the room.

When I was alone, I spent some time thinking over the incident. I was sincerely convinced that the truth of the matter was as I had said. No doubt Antonio had been excited by the contact with her arm and had been unable to control his excitement. But I was sure that he had done nothing to facilitate or repeat such contacts, which anyway, in the position he was in, were unavoidable. He was, in fact, to be blamed only for having failed to elude his involuntary desire. Such, moreover, is still my conviction, for I consider that certain temptations are all the stronger for being neither premeditated nor courted.

These considerations, made in solitude and in perfect good faith, dissipated the last of my remorse. I knew that, fundamentally, I had acted from selfishness; but this selfishness did not contradict what I held to be true justice. I was convinced of Antonio's innocence; and I therefore felt no scruple about placing my own convenience before what I judged to be a mere caprice on the part of my wife.

A few minutes later I joined Leda at table. She seemed perfectly calm, not to say serene. During a moment when the maid had gone out of the room with the dishes, she said to me: "All right . . . you can go on employing Antonio, but you must arrange things so that I don't see him. . . . If I even meet him on the stairs, I won't answer for myself. . . . You've been warned."

Filled with embarrassment, I pretended not to have heard. She added: "It may be that it's only a caprice . . . but my caprices ought to be more important to you than your own convenience, don't you think?"

It was just exactly the opposite of what I myself had decided; and I could not help making a mental note of it. It so happened that, at that moment, the maid came in again and the conversation dropped. Later, during our walk, I tried to resume it: I was feeling remorse again and I wanted her to be convinced of my reasons. But this time, to my surprise, she said gently: "Don't let's talk about it any more, Silvio, if you don't mind. This morning it seemed to matter a lot to me, I don't myself know why; but now, after having thought it over, I see that I was exaggerating. . . . I can assure you now that it no longer matters to me in the least. . . ."

She appeared sincere, and, in a way, to be almost sorry for her anger of the morning. "Are you quite sure?" I insisted.

"Yes, I swear," she said warmly; "what reason could I have for lying about it?"

I was silent; and we continued our walk talking of other things. And so I was convinced that my wife had really dismissed the subject from her mind.

8

TO-DAY, in relating the incident of Antonio, I cannot but portray it in the perspective of events that occurred before and after it. The same thing, I imagine, happens when one writes history. But, just as events, in reality extremely important, pass almost unnoticed by their contemporaries; just as very few, not merely among the spectators but even among the actors, realized that the French Revolution *was* the French Revolution; so, at the moment when it took place, the Antonio episode did not strike my imagination at all forcibly—much less so, in fact, than these notes might lead one to suppose. I was really not prepared to attach importance to an incident of that kind: my relations with my wife had hitherto been rational and happy; and nobody would expect to find a medieval trap-door in the middle of a bright modern room. I must insist on this quality of innocence in my mind at that moment: it partly excuses my selfishness and explains my superficiality. In fact, whatever the reasons were, I was neither willing nor able, on that occasion, to think evil. So much so that, next day, when Antonio knocked at my study door at the usual time, I realized that I felt neither resentment nor agitation. In the state of extreme objective mental detachment in which I found myself, it seemed almost a pleasure to study the man in the new light that my wife's accusations had thrown upon him. In the first place, while he was shaving me and while I, as usual, was talking to him (and it was no effort for me to talk to him),

I observed him closely. He was carefully intent, as always, upon his work and, as always, was doing his job lightly and skilfully. I thought to myself that, if my wife's accusations were true, it meant that he was exceptionally clever at dissimulation, so absorbed and so placid did that broad, rather plump face of his, with its cold yellowish-brown colour, appear to be. There still echoed in my ears those words of my wife's: "He's an outrageous, horrible, sinister man"—but after examining him with extreme care, I was forced to conclude that there was nothing outrageous, horrible, or sinister about him. If anything, he had rather a fatherly appearance, the appearance of a man accustomed to looking after five small children, an appearance of purely physical, unconscious authority. Another thought came into my mind as I looked at him, and though I recognized in a confused way that it was a foolish thought, I immediately seized upon it as upon an irrefutable argument: so ugly a man— unless he was mad, which Antonio certainly was not— could not hope to have any success with women, least of all with a woman like my wife, who was so beautiful and of a class so different from his. Not without satis-faction, I noted that he really was fat in the face, and with an unattractive kind of fatness which did not give an impression of good health either—rather greasy, smooth and a little flabby, and with an unwholesomely swollen appearance between jaw and neck which reminded one of the similar swelling that is to be seen in certain tropical snakes at moments of anger. He had large ears, with flat, pendulous lobes; and his bald head, burnt, perhaps, by the summer sun, was brown in patches. Antonio was evidently a very hairy man: tufts of hair sprouted from his ears and from his nostrils, and even his cheekbones and the tip of his nose were hairy. After examining this ugliness for a long time with complacent minuteness, I chose a moment when Antonio had turned away to wipe his razor on a piece of paper, to say, in a careless tone: "I've always wondered, Antonio, whether a man like you, married and with five children, can find the time and the opportunity to carry on with women."

He answered without smiling, turning back towards me with his razor: "For that particular thing, Signor Baldeschi, time can always be found."

I confess I had expected a different reply and I was considerably surprised. I objected: "But isn't your wife jealous?"

"All wives are jealous."

"So you're unfaithful to her?"

He lifted the razor and, looking me in the face, said: "Excuse me, Signor Baldeschi, but that is my business."

I felt myself blushing. I had put that indiscreet question to him because I thought, rather stupidly, that I had the right to do so, as a superior to an inferior; but he had put me, as they say, in my place, as an equal to an equal, and this I had not expected. I had a feeling of irritation and was almost tempted to answer: "It's not only your business but mine too, since you've had the impudence to annoy my wife." But I controlled this impulse and said rather confusedly: "You mustn't be offended, Antonio. . . . I didn't mean anything."

"Of course not," he said; and then, applying the razor to my cheek and slowly shaving me, he added, as though he wanted to mitigate the sharpness of his first remark and soothe my mortification: "Why, Signor Baldeschi, every-body likes women. . . . Even the priest over there at San Lorenzo has a woman, and that woman has presented him with two children. If you could look inside people's heads you'd see that everyone's got some woman or other . . . but no one wants to talk about them, because if you do, it gets known and then people start gossiping. . . . And women, as you know, only trust the ones who don't talk."

Thus he read me a lesson on the importance of secrecy in love affairs; leaving me in doubt, however, as to whether he belonged to the category of men who do not talk and who are trusted by women. I said nothing more about it that morning, but changed the conversation. But the suspicion had crept into my mind that, after all, my wife's accusations might have some foundation. In the afternoon, as happened regularly once a week, the farmer's eldest son, Angelo, came to go over the accounts with me. I shut myself up with him in the study and, after examining the accounts, brought the conversation round to Antonio, asking him if he knew him and what he thought of him. Angelo, a young peasant with fair hair and an expression which combined cunning with foolishness, answered with a slightly malevolent smile: "Yes, yes, we know him, we know him all right."

"It seems to me," I enquired, "or am I mistaken?— that you don't much care for Antonio."

After a moment's hesitation, he said: "As a barber— there's no doubt he's a good barber. . . ."

"But . . ."

"But he's a stranger here," continued Angelo, "and strangers have different ways, as everybody knows. . . .

Perhaps things are different, where he comes from. . . .
Certainly no one in these parts can abide him."

"Why?"

"Well—so many things. . . ." And Angelo smiled
again, shaking his head. It was a self-conscious, knowing
smile and yet full of dislike for Antonio, as though the
fault that the local people found with the barber was
something that had a funny side to it.

"What sort of things, for instance?" I asked.

I saw him grow serious; and then he answered, stressing
his words in a slightly unctuous way: "Well, you see,
Signor Baldeschi, in the first place he's always annoying
women. . . ."

"Really?"

"Ugh—and *how*! . . . you've no idea. . . . Pretty or
ugly, old or young, anything does for him. . . . And not
only in his shop, where they go to get their hair curled—
but outside it too, ask anyone you like. . . . On Sundays
he takes his bike and goes prowling round the countryside—as you might go out shooting . . . it's disgusting.
But I tell you, one of these days he's going to find someone who'll put a stop to his tricks. . . ." Having now
overstepped the limit of his usual reserve, Angelo had
become loquacious, adopting a sort of moralizing tone,
rather heavy and flattering, typical of a peasant who speaks
more or less as he imagines his landlord likes him to speak.

"What about his wife?" I asked, interrupting him.

"His poor wife, what can she do? She cries and gets
all worked up. . . . He's taught her to shave his clients
and every now and then he leaves her in charge of the
shop and gets out his bike and tells her he's going into

the town . . . but instead of that he goes round looking for a girl. Why, last year . . ."

I decided that Angelo had now given me all the information I needed; there was nothing more to be expected from him except more gossip about Antonio's shocking behaviour, and it seemed to me hardly dignified to drag it out of him and listen to it. And so I changed the conversation and soon afterwards sent him away.

When I was alone, I fell into a kind of thoughtful abstraction. So my wife had been right, or at least there was a strong probability that she had been right. This Antonio was a libertine, and it was even possible that he had actually tried to seduce my wife. I realized now that the mystery of Antonio—who did not seem to care much about his work, nor to be excessively fond of his family, nor interested in politics—did not exist. There was no mystery, and that was the whole mystery. Antonio was a commonplace Casanova, a perfectly ordinary fornicator. And those discreet, oily manners of his were the manners of a man who, as he himself had expressed it, was loved by women because he did not talk.

I had a strange feeling, almost of disappointment. At heart, and almost without realizing it, I had hoped that Antonio would not be so quickly and so easily deflated. I had liked Antonio, I now saw, just because there was in him—or so it had seemed to me—something mysterious. The mystery having been dispersed, nothing remained but a poor fellow who went about annoying women, *all* women, including, perhaps, women like my wife who were utterly out of his reach. There was something that irritated me in this discovery of the secret mainspring of the barber's life. Previously, if I had allowed myself to be infected by Leda's resentment, I might have hated him. Now that I knew all about him, however, I seemed to feel nothing except pity mingled with contempt—a feeling which was humiliating not only for him but for me also, since I now saw myself suddenly degraded to a mortifying rivalry with a village Don Juan.

And yet, strange to say, there persisted in me the conviction that he had not really dared to raise his eyes towards my wife; and that, as I had at first supposed, he had been led against his will to make his admiration clear to her in his own way. The fact that he was a libertine did not seem to me to destroy this supposition; it appeared, rather, to explain the facility with which he had become excited at the first chance contact—a facility easily understandable in an adolescent whose senses are always ready to trip him up, but unlikely in an experienced man of forty whose ardours may be supposed to have cooled. Only a libertine, accustomed to cultivate certain instincts to the exclusion of all others, could have a sensibility so prompt and so irresistible.

I went so far as to admit that, all things considered, he had not been altogether displeased at finding himself in that embarrassing situation and that he had at the same time both encouraged and fought against it. But there seemed to me to be no doubt at all that, in the first instance, it had been not deliberate but accidental.

It is possible that this inclination on my part to consider Antonio as being initially innocent (and I still consider him to be so), may have derived, partly at any rate, from my own selfishness, that is, from my fear of having to give him the sack and shave myself. But, even if this was true, I was certainly not aware of it. I thought over the whole affair with extreme objectivity; and often there is nothing like objectivity—that is, the forgetting of the links that connect objects and subjective motives—to encourage self-deception. To my conviction of Antonio's innocence, and to the feeling of contemptuous pity that I now had for him, must be added my wife's exaggerated reaction, which, if I had even imagined that I could be jealous, destroyed from the very first moment every reason for jealousy. In any case I am not of a jealous nature—at least, I do not think so. In me every passion is finally dissolved in the acid of reflection—a method as good as any other for subduing passion by destroying, at the same time, both its tyrannical power and the suffering it brings.

After my conversation with Angelo, I went as usual for a walk with my wife. It was then for the first time that I genuinely felt I was deceiving her. I felt I ought to tell her all I had learned about Antonio; but I didn't want to because I was aware that to do so would be, as it were, to rekindle in her, more strongly than ever, that first flame of anger that seemed now to be spent. Uncertain and filled with remorse, I at last said to her, at a moment when she appeared rather absent-minded: "Perhaps you're still thinking about Antonio's lack of respect? . . . If you really want me to, I'll get rid of him."

I think that, if she had asked it of me, this time I should have satisfied her. In effect, my selfishness had received a shock; and I only needed a little encouragement to give her what she wanted. I saw her give a start: ". . . Thinking about the barber? . . . no, no, not at all. . . . To

69

tell the truth I had really forgotten all about him."

"But if you want me to, I'll get rid of him," I insisted, encouraged by this indifference of hers which seemed to be quite sincere, and with the feeling of making a proposal that could not fail to be rejected.

"But I don't want you to," she said, "it doesn't matter to me in the least. . . . Really, as far as I'm concerned, it's just as if nothing had happened at all."

"You see, I was thinking . . ."

"It's a thing that concerns you and only you," she concluded with a thoughtful air, "for the reason that it's only you, now, who can be vexed, or not vexed, by his presence here. . . ."

"To tell the truth, it doesn't worry *me*."

"Well then, why should you get rid of him?"

I was pleased at this reasonableness on her part, although I was again conscious of a vague sort of disappointment. But it was my fate, at that period, that the happiness of a creative instinct at last satisfied should have made me fail to analyse carefully any of the feelings which, one after the other, manifested themselves in me. Next day Antonio came again and I noticed with astonishment that that curious charm of his, far from being dispelled by Angelo's information, still remained intact. In fact, the mystery of which I had been aware before I knew anything about him, subsisted even now that I thought I knew everything. This mystery had been thrust back into a less accessible region, that was all. The thought came to me that it was rather like the mystery of all other things, both great and small: everything about them can be explained except their existence.

9

DURING the days that followed I went on working
with an impetus and a facility that appeared to
increase steadily the nearer I approached the end
of my task. Antonio continued to come every morning,
and I, when that first embarrassment was over, regarded
him again with unimpaired curiosity. I felt that there was
now a bond between him and me; I might have severed
this bond at the very beginning, if I had dismissed him
as my wife had suggested; but I had not done this, and
a new relationship, tacit but recognizable, had resulted.
I find it difficult to explain the feeling that this relationship gave me. At first there had been, between me and
Antonio, the usual relationship that exists between
superior and inferior; after my wife's accusation this
relationship had been modified: the superior was also
the husband whose honour was assailed or who might
believe his honour to be assailed, the inferior was also
the assailant, or might believe himself to be the assailant.
But these two relationships were in fact purely conventional, founded as they were, the first on the fictitious
state of dependence and authority conferred by the giving
and taking of a wage, the second on the no less fictitious
moral obligation imposed by the matrimonial tie. In
suggesting that I should replace Antonio, my wife had
really suggested that I should accept these two conventions
without taking into account the particular, effective factors
in the case. I, however, had rejected her suggestion,

and Antonio had not been replaced. Now I felt that, as a consequence of my refusal, there had grown up between him and me a new relationship which was certainly much more real because it was founded upon the situation as it was and not as it ought to have been; only this relationship could be neither classified nor defined, and it made possible many consequences. I knew that, having refused to behave as anyone else in my place would have behaved—that is, as a superior and as a husband—I had opened the way to all sorts of possibilities, since everything now depended upon the developments in the real situation, independent of convention, in which we found ourselves. I saw that, in substance, the attitude suggested to me by my wife, conventional as it was, was the only tenable attitude if one wanted the situation to retain a recognizable external appearance. Outside this attitude anything was possible, and everything dissolved and fell to pieces. This attitude allowed each of us to keep to a well-known, pre-established role; outside this attitude our identities became blurred, misty, interchangeable.

These reflections made me understand the usefulness of moral standards and social conventions, which are, of course, external, but are indispensable for checking natural disorder and bringing it to order. And yet, on the other hand, I saw that, once moral standards and social conventions have been rejected, this same disorder must perforce tend to come to a standstill and systematize itself upon a foundation of sheer necessity. In other words, apart from the solution proposed by my wife, there remained one other solution which would be dictated by the actual nature of the circumstances. It was rather like a river which is either confined between artificial embankments or is allowed to spread out according to the slope and the accidents of the ground: in both cases, though by different methods and with different effects, it will form a bed of its own by which it may run away to the sea. But this second solution, the most natural and the most fateful, was still unlikely to come about, and, as it seemed to me, would perhaps never come about at all: Antonio would continue to come and shave me, I would finish my work and, later on, my wife and I would go away, and I would never know how much truth there had been in my wife's accusations. I can now set forth these reflections of mine in an orderly and lucid fashion. But, at the time, they were not so much reflections as vague feelings, and it was as though they proceeded from an indisposition caused by consciousness, which had taken the place of my previous agreeable unconsciousness.

It may perhaps seem surprising that I should have thought, or rather felt, in this way at the very moment when the thing was going on and was developing under my very eyes, and when my most precious affections were, or might seem to me to be, threatened. But I wish to repeat what I have already said more than once: I was absorbed in creative activity (or thought I was) and everything else was indifferent to me. Of course I had not ceased to love my wife and to have a natural sense of my own honour; but artistic creation, by a strange miracle, had removed the heavy stamp of urgency from these things and had transferred it to the pages of the book that I was engaged in writing. If my wife, instead of accusing Antonio of being disrespectful to her, had revealed to me that she had seen him wiping his razor on one of the pages of my story, I certainly should not have speculated upon his ignorance or his irresponsibility; I should have dismissed him at once. And yet such a fault was certainly more understandable, more justifiable, more pardonable than the fault that had been imputed to him. What was it that made me indifferent to what he had done in relation to my wife and, on the other hand, made me react so violently to the possibility of his spoiling my work? This was where the mystery came in of which I had been aware in him from the beginning, the mystery that Angelo's revelations had quite failed to dispel and which lay, in truth, more in myself than in him. It was a mystery, when all is said and done, that is created, and always will be created, every time that one leaves the surface of things and descends into the depths.

As for my wife, she no longer came and joined me, as before, while Antonio was shaving me, and I suppose that, until the barber had left the house, she remained shut up in her own room. In the end this attitude of hers annoyed me because it showed that she was clinging to her first conventional reaction and had no intention of exchanging it for an approach such as mine, rational, speculative. I asked her—I do not remember how, or on what occasion—why she never appeared now during the morning. She answered me directly, without any irritation but with just a touch of impatience: "But, Silvio . . . really sometimes I almost doubt your intelligence . . . how could I possibly appear? That man hasn't been punished for his insolence. . . . If I appeared he might think I had forgiven him—or worse. . . . By not appearing I allow him to think that I preferred to avoid a scandal and so didn't tell you."

I don't know what demon of subtlety prompted me to reply: "He may also have thought that you didn't notice. . . . And this makes it worse; you're allowing him to think that you did notice and that, in spite of that, you're not doing anything about it or making me do anything."

"The only possible thing," she answered calmly, "would have been to give him the sack that same day."

10

AT last the morning came when I wrote the last word at the end of the last line of the last page, and closed the exercise-book which contained my story. It seemed to me that I had made an enormous effort and that I had been working for an infinite time: in point of fact I had jotted down the equivalent of about a hundred printed pages and had worked for little more than twenty days or so. With my exercise-book in my hand I went over to the window and mechanically turned over its pages: tears came into my eyes, whether from joy or from exhaustion at the end of my labours, I did not know. I could not help thinking that in that bundle of sheets was harvested the finest product of my life, everything, in fact, that from henceforth would make life seem worth while, for the past as well as for the future. I turned the pages slowly, and as I gazed at them I became aware that my sight was growing dim and I felt the tears falling upon my hands. Then I saw Antonio crossing the gravel sweep on his bicycle, and hastily I replaced the exercise-book on the desk and wiped my eyes.

Later, after Antonio had left, I went into my bedroom and, while dressing, I started as usual to think about the work I had done. On other days I had been used to think merely of the pages I had written that same morning, but this day, for the first time, I gloated over the whole story, caressing it in my memory from beginning to end. There in front of me, in fact, was what I now privately called my masterpiece, complete and perfect, and I was at last able to enjoy it in its entirety as one enjoys a panoramic view after a long and wearisome climb during which one has been able to catch only partial glimpses of it. But these things can only be suggested, not described. All I can say is that, while I was thinking about my story, time seemed to be suspended in a sort of ravishment—and so, indeed, it was. All of a sudden the door opened and my wife appeared on the threshold: "What on earth are you doing?" she said. "Lunch is ready . . . it's been ready for three quarters of an hour."

I was sitting on the bed, in my dressing-gown, and my clothes were still lying on the chair on which I had placed them the night before. I looked at the watch on my wrist: Antonio had left at about a quarter to one, and now it was two o'clock. I had spent a whole hour and a quarter sitting on the bed, with one sock on and the other in my hand. "I'm sorry," I said, with a violent start of surprise, "I don't know what can have happened to me . . . I'll come at once." I dressed hurriedly and joined her downstairs.

In the afternoon, when that first enthusiasm had subsided, the first questions took shape in my mind. I had decided to read the story to my wife as soon as I had finished it. I trusted her more than I trusted myself, more than I trusted any critic whatsoever. As I have already said, she was not a cultivated woman, she had no knowledge of literary matters, and her interest in books was the interest of an ordinary person who pays more attention to facts than to style. But, just for these reasons, just because I knew that her judgment would be more or less that of the ignorant public, I trusted her. I knew her to be lively, sufficiently intelligent, full of good sense, and, in the long run, incapable of being taken in, though for different reasons from those of a professional man of letters. Her judgment, I was aware, would not perhaps be competent to give me an idea of the strictly literary value of the story, but would certainly enable me to understand whether the book was alive or not. And after all, in the case of any book whatsoever, the first question to be considered should be that of its vitality as a whole. There are books that are extremely imperfect, badly constructed, jumbled, untidy and yet alive, which we read and shall always read; and there are, on the other hand, books that are perfect in every detail, well planned, well composed, tidy and polished and yet dead, which, with all their perfection, not knowing what to make of it, we reject utterly. This was a conviction I had reached after many years of reading and of practice in criticism. And so, in the first place, I had to know whether my book was alive; and nobody would be able to assure me of this better than my wife.

I ought to say that I prepared myself for this trial—which, in a way, I considered to be of supreme importance—with complete tranquillity of mind. I still had many doubts about the literary qualities of my story, not having re-read it and having, also, the impression that I had perhaps written it in rather a hurry. But with regard to its vitality it seemed to me that there could be no doubts. Had not all those discouraging feelings of sterility, of strain, of inadequacy, of bungling, of sophistry, which had tormented me all my life and which had always, in the end, brought me to a standstill whenever I had tried to write—had not all these gradually fallen away, the further I progressed in my composition? Had I not been conscious, as I wrote, that a kind of dam had burst in my breast, and that all that it had been holding back had escaped, not to run away quietly like a brook but forcing its way out and swelling like a flood? Had I not, indeed, felt all the time that my essential self was faithfully reflected in what I was writing, as was all that I wrote in my essential self? Other and similar arguments had by now brought me to face with tranquillity any effects that the reading of my story might have upon my wife.

There were still one or two practical difficulties. The manuscript, though not inextricably confused, contained numbers of crossings-out and additions between the lines which might perhaps make the reading of it somewhat muddled and unpleasing. It might happen that, at certain points, I would have to stop and examine the page in order to pick up the lost thread of meaning, thus breaking a charm which I would wish to be uninterrupted and complete. It might also have happened that, in the hurry of this first draft, certain details, certain finishing touches, might have been forgotten. While on a walk with Leda, talking of indifferent matters, I debated the pros and cons of reading the story to her that same afternoon. I decided finally that I must put off the reading for about ten days, during which time I would type out the manuscript. I knew that, as I copied it, many things that might be wrong would come right, and many others that might be lacking altogether could be added. The style would thus be consolidated and all raggedness would be eliminated. Besides—and this was a decisive argument—I would be able, for another ten days, to enjoy my masterpiece in unpublished intimacy. This last reason finally convinced me.

I had brought my typewriter with me from Rome; it was a new one, or nearly so, for I had used it only for writing business letters and an occasional article. It was an American machine, of the best and most up-to-date kind that could be found, and its high qualities, during my periods of sterility, had sometimes filled me with bitterness. I was, it seemed to me, merely one of those wealthy, incompetent writers who possess everything needed for the writing of a masterpiece—money, time, a comfortable, quiet study, paper of the finest quality, fountain pens of the best make, the last word in typewriters—everything except genius. Such a man comes finally to envy the cheap note-book in which some starving youth scribbles a few lines, every now and then, in pencil, as the fleeting inspiration moves him, sitting in the corner of a café or a popular eating-house. Now, however, the bitter sense of sterility aroused in me by my beautiful typewriter and all the other conveniences at my disposal, had disappeared. I had wealth, I had leisure— but I had created; expensive paper, a study, a library, a typewriter were all mine—but I had created. Such superstitions, I believe, fill the lives of men who create —or who think they create.

But when I went, that same afternoon, to examine my typewriter and see that all was in order, I discovered that I had left my typewriting paper behind in Rome. I knew that there was no question of being able to find this sort of paper in the village; so I decided to go and buy some in the town. There was a stationer's shop there that supplied all the offices of the neighbourhood. It was, however, impossible for me to go there that day, since the farmer's one-horse trap, my only available means of transport, had already gone out in the morning. I planned to go next day. That same evening I announced my intended expedition to my wife, telling her that I had to go into the town for some shopping but not specifying what it was I meant to buy; and, as a matter of form, I suggested that she should accompany me. I say "as a matter of form" because I knew that there was not much room in the trap and that she did not care for that slow and uncomfortable vehicle. In any case I was not sorry that she should not come: I was so happy that solitude seemed to me preferable to company. As I had foreseen, she refused, without even the slightest comment upon the purpose of my expedition. She asked, after a moment: "What time will you be back?"

"Quite soon . . . at any rate for lunch."

She was silent, and then went on, in a casual way: "What's to be done if the barber comes?"

I thought for a moment, and then answered: "I shall certainly be back before he comes. . . . If by any chance I'm late, ask him to wait." This reply was dictated by my dislike of having to make use of one of the barbers in the town, and of their razors which were used on other customers. Antonio brought with him nothing at all; all the required implements were supplied by me.

She said nothing, and we changed the conversation. Now that my work was finished I felt my love for my wife coming back as strong as before, and even stronger. Or rather, I had loved her all the time, but, during those twenty days of work, I had, so to speak, suspended the expression of my love. We were sitting at table, in the little dining-room. Leda, as usual, was in evening dress, in a graceful white gown with long, flowing lines, low at the back and, with its simple draperies, rather like a Greek *peplum*. Round her neck, upon her fingers, and in the lobes of her ears were her jewels, all of them massive and of great value. The parchment-shaded lamp in the middle of the table lit up her face with a soft, golden light. Her face was expertly made up; and she had retained the short, curly *coiffure* that Antonio had devised for her. I noticed for the first time that her long, thin face, now that it had ceased to be enclosed between loose, trailing locks of hair, had assumed a quite different aspect from the one I was accustomed to: it appeared younger, less wistful, and had about it a look of cruel, archaic sensuality. No longer softened and caressed by the waving hair, the strained, unmoving slant of her enormous blue eyes, the sharp sensitiveness of her nostrils, the smiling bigness of her mouth—all were fully revealed. She seemed to have been stripped of something and therefore to be more real, with an antique, satyr-like appearance which reminded one at the same time of primitive Greek sculptures with set expressions of ironical ambiguity upon their brows, and of a goat's Semitic profile. To emphasize this appearance my wife, as on the day of the Antonio incident, had fastened above her left temple, on the gold of her hair, a bunch of fresh, red flowers. Looking at her, I said: "You know, after all, your hair as Antonio arranged it really suits you very well. . . . I've only just noticed it."

She seemed to give an almost imperceptible start at the name of the barber and lowered her eyes. With her long fingers she was twisting the massive crystal stopper of a decanter, and between her pointed nails, red as rubies. the faceted stopper looked, in the lamplight, like an enormous diamond shot through with gleaming lights. She said slowly: "The idea of doing my hair like this wasn't Antonio's, it was mine. . . . All he did was to do what I told him—and badly, too."

"And how did you come to think of it?"

"I used to wear it like this when I was a girl, very many years ago," she said. "It's an arrangement that suits either very young women, or"—and she smiled slightly—"middle-aged ones, like me."

"What d'you mean, middle-aged? Don't say such silly things. . . . And those flowers suit you perfectly. . . ."

The maid came in and we helped ourselves in silence. Then, when she had left the room again, I put down my knife and fork and said: "You look like a different person . . . or rather, you're yourself all the time, but with a new appearance." All at once I felt deeply disturbed, and I added in a whisper: "You're very beautiful, Leda . . . it may be that I forget that, every now and then . . . but the moment always comes when I realize how utterly in love with you I am."

She went on eating and did not reply; but there was no sign of disdain, in fact a certain satisfaction was visible in the faint quiver of her nostrils and the droop of her lowered eyelids. It was her way of accepting compliments that were agreeable to her and I knew it. All at once there came over me an indescribable turmoil of love. I placed my hand on hers and murmured: "Give me a kiss."

She raised her eyes, looked at me, and asked, with simplicity and perhaps without any intended irony: "Is your work finished, then?"

"No," I lied, "but I can't look at you without loving you and without wanting to kiss you. . . . To hell with my work."

As I said this I pulled her by the arm so that she leant over in my direction. She resisted, frowning, with an air half serious, half tempted, and said briefly, in a voice full of love: "You're crazy"; then turning suddenly gave me the kiss I had asked for, abruptly, impetuously, but with sincerity. We kissed in breathless haste, crushing our lips violently against each other's; it was like the kiss of two ingenuous but ardent youngsters who are not yet expert in love and who spoil their own enjoyment by nervousness and impatience. And I, in that fleeting kiss—which I seemed to be snatching rather than merely receiving from my wife's lips—felt that I had in truth gone back to my boyhood and that I was in danger of being surprised by a stern mother instead of a devoted old servant who would be both embarrassed and sympathetic. Immediately after the kiss we became composed again, just like two children; she serene and quiet, I a little out of breath. But the maid did not come; and I looked at my wife and then I managed to laugh, both at myself and at her, and I laughed and slapped her hand. This made her suspicious and she asked: "Why are you laughing?"

"I'm sorry," I said. "I'm not laughing at you. . . . I'm laughing because I'm happy."

With her eyes lowered, and in a calm, conversational tone, as she went on eating, she asked: "And what is it that makes you so happy?"

This time I could resist no longer and I said, ingenuously: "For the first time in my life I have everything I wanted, and what's more—a thing which is much rarer—I know that I have it. . . ."

"What was it you wanted?"

"For years and years," I said, "I've wanted to love a woman and to be loved by her in return. . . . Well, now I love you, and you, I believe, love me. For years and years I've had an ambition to write something lasting, something alive, something poetical. . . . Now that I've finished my story, I can say that I've achieved that too."

I had decided not to speak to my wife about the story until I had finished copying it. But my joy was so great that I couldn't resist it. Her reaction to the news surprised me, although I knew that she loved me and took a lively interest in all that I did. "You've finished?" she exclaimed with a delight that was flattering because sincere, "you've finished?"—and her voice had a clear ring in it which enchanted me—"Oh, Silvio—and you never told me anything about it!"

"I didn't tell you about it," I explained, "because, although in the strict sense of the word I've finished, I've still got to type out the manuscript. . . . I shan't really have finished till the day when I've finished the typing."

"That doesn't matter," she said, with that same complete and flattering spontaneity, "you've finished and this is a great moment. . . . We must drink to the health of your book."

85

Her manner was charmingly, impetuously affectionate and her blue eyes, so beautiful and so luminous, rested seductively upon me as though they wanted to caress me. With a hand that trembled slightly I poured some wine into our glasses. Then we raised them high above the table. "To you and to your book," she said in a low voice, looking at me. I drank, and saw her drink, and then she put down her glass and leant towards me offering her lips; and this time it was a true kiss, long and passionate, and it was only after we had finished kissing that we noticed that the maid had come in and was looking at us, leaning against the sideboard with the tray in her hands.

"Come on, Anna, you must drink too; this is a great day," said my wife with that graceful, authoritative naturalness with which she knew so well how to deal with the most embarrassing social situations. "Silvio, give Anna some wine. Come on, Anna, drink Signor Silvio's health." The old woman demurred, smiling ironically. "Well, well, if it's a health to be drunk . . ." she said then; and, putting down the tray on the sideboard, she took the glass, raised it with an awkward gesture and drank the toast. My wife, with the same naturalness of manner, then helped herself and started eating again, still continuing to question me, in a simple way, about my work. "And this time." she asked, "are you really certain that you've done something good?"

"Yes," I answered, "as far as one can be certain with this kind of thing . . . and I can be more certain than many other people might be, because I'm not a bad critic myself—of that, at least, I'm perfectly certain."

"You know, I want to tell you how very pleased I am," she went on after a brief silence, placing her hand on mine and looking into my face. I lifted her hand and kissed it. I was infinitely grateful to my wife for the way in which she had welcomed the news of the finishing of my work, by which she had once again revealed to me, as by an infallible touchstone, the pure gold of the feeling that she cherished towards me. I felt, also, intoxicated by the delight she showed, just as though that welcome had come from the most exacting of critics instead of from an ignorant outsider like herself. It was a callow feeling, but I believe that all writers, even the most sophisticated, experience it at least once in their lives, at the beginning of their careers, at a time when they are timid, though hopeful, candidates for the opinion of some more important, older colleague. Uplifted by this joyful atmosphere, I discovered all of a sudden that, without my being aware of it, we had finished our meal, had risen from the table, had walked into the drawing-room, and that my wife was standing in front of me pouring out the coffee.

I do not remember clearly the details of what happened that night, just as one does not remember people's faces and expressions when a sudden flash of lightning dazzles everybody with its blinding glare. I only remember that I was excited, hilarious, in a state of exaltation, and that I talked about my future and hers. Then I explained how it had happened that I had written the story. Taking us two and our marriage as subject, I analysed the material I had made use of, and described to her the changes and the profundities I had introduced into it. I also quoted other famous books, making comparisons, tracing precedents, linking up my own work with a tradition. Every now and then I broke off into sidelines of reflection or anecdote. Finally I picked up a book, an anthology which had recently appeared, and read aloud some poems by modern authors. My wife was sitting on the sofa, beautiful, elegant, her legs crossed and one silver-shod foot raised, smoking and listening to me; and I was aware that she was following all that I said with the same affection, truly as unchangeable as gold, that she had displayed to me with such spontaneity when I had announced that I had finished my story. Alone in that nineteenth-century drawing-room, amongst all those pieces of antiquated and creaking furniture, in that isolated villa in the depths of the country, we enjoyed—at least I enjoyed—two hours of incomparable intimacy. And then, exactly at the moment when I was finally closing the anthology, the lights went out.

It was no rare thing, in that part of the country, for the electric light to fail: it was the time of the olive-harvest and the current would be diverted to the presses. In the darkness I went over to the french window that gave on to the gravelled space in front of the house and threw it wide open. The drive was white in the moonlight, and behind the black trees which framed it the night sky, too, was silvered by the full moon. On the threshold I stood still, searching for the moon itself but unable to find it. Then, all of a sudden, turning, I saw it rising rapidly behind the mountain on whose top stood the ancient town, at first no more than a segment, then, as though pushed upwards by some irresistible movement, becoming steadily larger and rounder until it hung, complete, a solid globe bathed in silver light, in a brightened sky. Its rays, falling vertically upon the brown walls of the town, threw them into crumbling relief, imparting to them a quality of coldness and loneliness. They seemed to acquire an air of fearless expectation, of vigilant guardianship, as in the days when they had been raised with the true purpose of defending the town; and I forgot myself as I looked at them and as I looked at the moon hanging above them. Then, from the room behind, came the voice of my wife who had remained sitting on the sofa: "Don't you think it's time to go to bed? It must be getting very late, you know."

It was, possibly, a suggestion that we should merely go to our beds and sleep. But I, in my exalted state of mind, took it as a love invitation and turned hastily back into the room, saying: "There's a magnificent moon . . . why shouldn't we go for a little walk?" Without a word my wife obeyed me and came forward out of the darkness of the room, and I was pleased by this docile agreement of hers. We went out together on to the gravelled space in front of the house.

The silence was profound, as it is on these autumn nights when all the insects of summer have retreated into silence until the following year. The two plaster dogs that gazed at the villa from the edges of the open space seemed also a part of this silence, lively, almost affectionate in their attitudes, but white and dumb. We started off down the drive, beneath the low vault of trees. While we were in this deep shadow, I put my arm round Leda's waist and felt her lean back against it lazily, gracefully, without trace of sentimentality, as though my gesture had been foreseen and already discounted. Thus linked together, we walked on down the drive, between the two slanting rows of trees whose trunks and foliage were flecked here and there with uncertain gleams of white by the moonlight as it filtered through the tangled undergrowth. We walked the whole length of the drive and, at a short distance from the gate, turned off into another path, between two rows of cypresses. Beyond the cypresses one could catch a glimpse of the wide plain, silent in the moonlight, and, at the top of the path, where there was a silvery emptiness, one could divine a further stretch of open country. My wife was leaning against my arm and I could feel, through her dress, the soft curve of her waist where it joined the roundness of her hip. At the end of the path we turned off along a track which divided the park from the fields. The park came to a natural end here in the open country: the last trees stretched out their boughs across the track to the first rows of vines. A little further on, on the top of a hill, were the farm buildings, whose rustic front, brilliantly lit by the moon, could already be partly seen. The track, still skirting the edge of the park, passed below the farm buildings, rounded a knoll upon which was a threshing-floor and three straw-stacks, and then lost itself in the countryside.

We walked slowly, with the trees of the park on one side and, on the other, the grassy slope of the hill. We passed the farm buildings and reached a point just below the threshing-floor; then I raised my eyes towards the three stacks. One of them was complete, made of fresh straw, of a bright, shining yellow; another was brown, the straw older; of the third there remained only a section, shaped like a rudder, against the crooked pole which had supported it. The moonlight, falling upon the three stacks and outlining their masses sharply against the dark, empty background of the open countryside, seemed to isolate them upon their knoll: the way they were placed, which was obviously not by mere chance, their monumental aspect, made one forget their real nature and suggested the idea of some mysterious under-lying purpose. I could not help thinking of the circles of enormous upright stones left by the Druids here and there on the plains of France and England. I said to my wife that the three stacks standing there in the brilliant light of the full moon reminded me of the dolmens of Brittany, and I went on to explain something of the pagan rites that were celebrated in those pre-historic temples. For an idea had come to me, or rather a desire—to climb up on to the threshing-floor with Leda and make love to her there, on the straw, on the ground, in the moonlight. In that way would I solemnize, in a worthy setting, the end of my work and, at the same time, our return to conjugal love. I do not say that certain literary memories did not enter into this desire; but, after all, I was a literary man, and it was right that literature, in me, should be fused with the deepest and most genuine impulses. In any case, I had a real longing for Leda, and the idea of making love to her in the open air, on a night of full moon, seemed to me absolutely natural and just such as might have occurred to a simpler, less cultivated man than myself.

I TOLD her that I wanted to climb up to the threshing-
floor and look at the immensely wide view that could
be obtained from there; she agreed and, still linked
together, we scrambled up the steep slope, over the
slippery grass. When we reached the threshing-floor we
stood quite still for a moment gazing at the landscape.
The whole wide plain stretched away as far as the eye
could see, in the clear night, and the moonlight, falling
upon that vast area of growing things, showed up the
rows of fruit-trees, the hedges, the empty spaces of the
fields, the vineyards. Here and there its brilliance was
concentrated upon the front of some farmhouse, bathing
it in silver. At the horizon, a row of black mountains
made a clear line between earth and the tranquil sky. A
far-away murmur, as of a train running hidden amongst
the cultivated fields, passed across the sleeping countryside and emphasized its vastness and its silence.

My wife gazed at this landscape almost in bewilder-
ment, as though she wished to penetrate the secret of its
serenity and its silence; and I, putting my arm round her
waist again, began talking to her in a low voice, pointing
out now one place, now another, in the plain below us,
and exalting the beauty of the night. Then, as we still
conversed together, I made her turn round towards the
mountain that rose behind us and pointed out the walls
of the town upon its top. We had moved, as we talked,
close to one of the straw-stacks: on the ground there was

scattered straw where the farmer's children played in the daytime. Suddenly I embraced her, murmuring: "Leda . . . isn't it better here than in your room?" And as I spoke I tried to push her gently to the ground.

She looked at me, her shining blue eyes dilated by a sudden temptation. Then, resisting me, she said: "No . . . the straw isn't clean. . . . Besides, it's so prickly. . . . I should ruin my frock."

"What does your frock matter?"

"Your work isn't finished yet," she said all of a sudden, with a laugh that was unexpected and full of coquettishness; "the day you've really finished it, we'll come back here, at night. . . . Is that all right?"

"No, it's not all right, there won't be any moon then. . . . To-night."

Softly, and as though she were still hesitating, she said: "Let me go, Silvio"; and then, all at once, she freed herself and ran off, down the hill, laughing. It was a fresh, childish laugh, full of an affectionate nervousness in which there seemed still to be a tremor of the temptation that I had discerned, a moment before, in her eyes; and this seemed to recompense me for the way in which it repulsed me. Perhaps it was better that it should have happened like this, I thought as I ran after her: a gentle refusal and a gracious laugh. She was running in front of me along the path between the park and the vineyards, but I caught her up easily and took her in my arms. But now I felt that that laugh had satisfied every desire of mine; and, after kissing her, I started walking along beside her, holding her hand tightly. The moonlight threw our two shadows in front of us—separate, but with the hands joined; and this chaste return of ours now appeared to me more truly loving than the embrace which she had evaded at the threshing-floor. We walked the whole length of the drive and reached the front of the house. The electric light had come on again in the meantime, and the french window of the drawing-room had a bright and welcoming look. We went into the house, and straight upstairs. She walked in front of me up the stairs and never had she looked so beautiful to me as in that soft, graceful movement of ascent which showed off the lines of her figure. On the landing she said again, in a characteristically jocular, and at the same time sensual, manner: "Finish your work, then . . . and we'll go together to the threshing-floor." I kissed her hand and went to my room. Very soon afterwards I was asleep.

Next morning my feeling of exaltation, far from having evaporated, had perhaps reached its highest point. My wife was still asleep when I climbed into Angelo's trap and drove off with him towards the town. Angelo perhaps thought it his duty to talk to me of the state of affairs of the countryside; and I let him chatter away almost without listening to him, being absorbed in my thoughts, or rather in my feelings. The trap started off down the drive, where the first rays of the morning sun were already playing, skirted the old boundary wall and turned into the main road. The air was mild, and the soft splendour of autumn lay upon all things; I looked round over the countryside, already partly despoiled and weary-looking, and all about me, in that accurate light, so different from the devouring glare of summer, all things

were clearly visible, each thing could be clearly distin-
guished, even to the finest detail and the subtlest shade of
colour; and I could not have enough of looking. Here was
a red leaf which, at a breath of wind, detached itself from
the bough of a vine; there a changing network of light
and faint shadow upon an old brown, green and grey
wall; farther on a lark, rising from the road almost under
the horse's hoofs, punctured space with brief flights and
came to rest beside a clod of earth in a bare field, and the
clod had been freshly turned and still had upon it the
gloss of the spade. There were patches of verdigris, of a
poisonous blue, upon the white walls of farm buildings;
there was moss, yellow as gold, on the weathered roof-
tiles of a little church that looked like a barn; there were
big, pale green acorns amongst the darker leaves of a
young oak that hung out over the road from the field
beside it. I rejoiced in these and other similar minute
details as though they had been rich with some ineffable
meaning; and I was aware that I owed this new way of
looking at things, as though I were in love with them, to
my own happiness, which, also, was new and ineffable.

After crossing part of the flat plain, the road attacked
the mountain slope, rising gently but unceasingly. The
trap proceeded at walking pace. I looked then for the
first time at the ancient walls rising sheer on the moun-
tain-top, brown but with edges glowing in the sunlight;
and all at once I felt myself flooded with an uncontrollable rapture, as though those walls had been the goal,
now at last visible, not of my brief morning expedition
but of my whole life. The trap climbed slowly, and I, for
a moment, as I looked at the walls, saw myself not as I

was, a mass of confused and transient thoughts and feelings, but firmly established in time, wearing, like a mantle, the predestined, the mysteriously simple, character that history attributes to its heroes. Thus, beneath this same sun, on a morning like this, along just such a road, had moved those great men, the bringers of consolation, whom I admired; and in this certainty I seemed to find confirmation that I myself, perhaps, would one day become one of these men. I seemed to divine it in the intensity of that moment as I lived it; it seemed to me the clearest possible sign of my entry into greatness and into eternity. I was surprised to find myself murmuring: "The twenty-seventh of October nineteen hundred and thirty-seven," over and over again, in time to the hard, insistent, regular beat of the horse's hoofs as it mounted the hill, and I had the feeling that the magic charm of that date, as I pronounced each of its syllables distinctly, already held in itself some sort of foreboding.

Our slow progress had brought us by now to the town gate, which consists of enormous masses of Etruscan masonry surmounted by a slender medieval arch. It stood golden in the sunshine; peasants driving donkeys or carrying baskets went through it in front of us: and it was, in fact, a morning just like any other morning, on top of this mountain as elsewhere. After we had passed the gate, my mood of exaltation fell suddenly flat as the trap went up over the cobbles of a steep street, between two rows of old houses. When we reached the main square I got down, asking Angelo to meet me there in an hour's time, and I went off to look for the paper I needed. The shop that I had in mind was further on along the Corso, and I had little difficulty in finding it. But I discovered to my surprise that the stationer kept no typewriting paper, only foolscap. I resigned myself disgustedly to buying a hundred of these double sheets, thinking that I could cut them up and make two sheets out of each. With my roll of paper under my arm I then went into the principal café and drank a vermouth, standing at the bar: it was an old-fashioned café, dark and dusty, with few bottles, of dubious aspect, upon the bar shelves, and no customers on the red divans round the walls. I left the café, returned to the square, went over to the newspaper kiosk and, after examining at length the four or five illustrated magazines and comic papers hung up there, I bought the morning paper and went and sat down on the stone seat in front of the Town Hall, beneath the convoluted coats-of-arms of extinct noble families and the iron rings for tying up horses. I was sorry now that I had told Angelo to come back in an hour's time, but consoled myself with the thought that he had things to do and that I should anyhow have had to wait for him. The irregular *piazza*, narrow, surrounded by medieval palaces, half in sunshine and half in shadow, was deserted, since it was not market-day: during the space of an hour and more that I remained there I cannot have seen more than ten people or so go past, of whom at least half were priests. I read the newspaper right through and realized that I was not in the least disturbed at having to wait, since my work was so satisfactorily finished and I should not in any case have started the typing that morning. I felt calm and in a perfectly normal state of mind, and when I had finished

97

the paper I started watching the numerous artisans who were at work in their shops all round the square. Meanwhile the sun was climbing higher and the shadow of the Town Hall, with its severe outline, grew less as it retreated across the cobble-stones. From somewhere or other a bell—a convent-bell, perhaps—began to ring violently; and this was at once followed by the graver tones of the bells in the tower of the principal church. It was noon; the whole town seemed to re-awake, and groups of people came into the *piazza*. I too, moved. I went slowly down the entire length of the Corso to the public gardens, a sunny meeting-place where I thought I might find Angelo. And there, in fact, he was, in the midst of a discussion with some country people. We started off at once on our homeward journey.

On the way back, perhaps owing to fatigue, my thoughts assumed a more rational turn. I began, I remember, to think about the publisher whom I should prefer to publish the book, about the binding I should choose, the critics who would write about it, and who would like it and who would not. Then I thought of Leda, and I said to myself that I had been very lucky to find her, and, perhaps for the first time since our marriage, it dawned upon my mind how fragile was the link that bound us. I was almost frightened when I thought how my whole life depended upon her feelings for me and mine for her, how everything might change and how I might lose her. My spirit was troubled at this thought, to the point of anguish; and, feeling my breath fail and my heart tremble, I understood how closely I was now bound to Leda and how I could no longer get on without her. I realized that, in possession of her, I felt myself to be so rich that I sometimes thought I would be able to live without her; but as soon as I imagined myself separated from her, I saw that I should be the most helpless, the most wretched, the most forlorn of men. And this separation might come about any day. All at once I felt utterly depressed and—though the sun was hot —chilled and shuddering from head to foot; my eyes filled with tears and I knew I was growing pale. Almost hysterically I ordered Angelo to quicken the horse's pace: "Good God!" I cried angrily, "we shan't be home till evening, at this rate." Luckily we had by now reached the flat ground, and the horse, knowing its stable was near, broke into a quick trot. I started watching the road anxiously, longing to reach home as soon as possible and to see Leda and find her just as I had left her. Here was the first stretch of main road across open country, then the second, beyond the bridge; and here at last was the final stretch of road along the wall that skirted the park. Here was the gate, and here was the drive. The open space in front of the house was full of sunshine, and on the threshold of the french window, just as though she had been waiting for me there for years—an almost incredible sight after my recent terror—was Leda, in a light-coloured dress, a book in her hand. I noticed with delight, from a long way off, her attitude of expectation: evidently she had settled down to read in the drawing-room, leaving the french window open, and at the sound of the trap wheels on the gravel of the drive had at once come out to meet me. The trap stopped, I jumped out and, after greeting her, went into the house.

"It's late," she said, following me; "the barber's been here quite a long time. He's waiting for you upstairs."

"What time is it?" I asked.

"It's after one."

"It was Angelo's fault," I said; "I'll go at once and get shaved and come down again."

She said nothing and went out into the garden. I rushed up the stairs, four at a time, and went into the study. Antonio stood waiting for me beside the table upon which the razors were laid out; he welcomed me with a good-morning and a slight bow. In a mad hurry I said to him: "Quick, Antonio . . . it's very late. Be as quick as you can," and threw myself into the armchair.

I realized now that I was in a hurry mainly because I was hungry. In the early morning I had had nothing but a cup of coffee, my stomach was empty and my head felt dizzy, and my hunger brought with it a kind of irritability which soon showed itself when Antonio, with his usual slowness, began to unfold the towel to put it round my neck. "Why can't he make haste?" I thought; "I told him I was in a hurry. . . . Devil take him." The composure of Antonio's movements, which formerly had so much pleased me, had now become hateful. I should have liked to tell him to hurry, but since I had already done so I saw that I could not repeat myself and this irritated me afresh. As he turned his back upon me and began stirring the brush round in the wooden soap-bowl, I followed his movements with an impatient eye, counting the seconds. My haste and my hunger increased simultaneously.

When he had worked the soap into a good lather, Antonio, holding the brush up in the air, turned to me and began soaping my face. He was unsurpassed in the art of concentrating upon his client's face a whole enormous mass of thick, white foam; but that morning his skilfulness irritated me. Every time the brush circled my cheek I thought it was for the last time, but always I was wrong: catching, with the point of his brush, a flake of froth that threatened to fall, Antonio would begin all over again, always with the same regular movement, to work up the lather on my face. I do not know why, but the idea of lying there in the armchair with froth all over my face gave me a feeling of absurdity; and—even worse—it almost seemed to me that Antonio consciously intended to make me look absurd.

This last suspicion was ridiculous and I immediately rejected it; but it shows how my hunger had upset me. At last, as the movement of the brush over my cheeks seemed to be going on for ever, I exclaimed angrily: "I told you to hurry up . . . and you go on and on soaping my face." I saw Antonio throw me a quick glance out of those round, bright, astonished eyes of his, and then, without a word, he put down the brush in the bowl and took up the razor.

But, before he turned away and after I had spoken, he had not been able to resist a final whisk to the lather on my right cheek. I noted this gesture of his as an act of disobedience which, I felt, came very near to insolence, and my irritation grew.

He took a moment to strop the razor, then bent over me and started shaving me. With his usual lightness and skill he removed the greater part of the lather from my right cheek, and then stretched forward to start on the left. In so doing, he pressed with his body against my arm, and I, for the first time since he had been shaving me, was aware of this pressure and at the same time could not help remembering Leda's accusations. There was no doubt about it, as he bent over me he pressed his body against my arm and shoulder, and I, at this contact, was conscious of a feeling of frantic repugnance. I could feel the softness of the lower part of his stomach, which I pictured to myself as hairy, muscular and sweaty, and enveloped in linen of a doubtful cleanliness; and all at once, through my own shudder of disgust, I seemed to understand that of my wife. It was a disgust of a particular kind, such as is inspired by this type of promiscuous, sensual contact which, though entirely casual, cannot but arouse, because of some quality in itself, the suspicion that it is deliberate.

I waited a moment, hoping that he would move. But he did not, nor, indeed, could he; and suddenly my disgust overcame my prudence. With a quick movement I drew back. At the same moment I felt the coldness of the razor as it cut into my cheek.

Immediately, from whence I know not, there descended upon me a fury of hatred against Antonio. He had at once drawn back the razor and was looking at me in astonishment. I leapt to my feet, raising my hand to my cheek from which blood was already spurting, and shouted: "What on earth are you doing? Are you mad?"

"But, Signor Baldeschi," he said, "you moved . . . you moved violently."

"That's not true," I yelled.

"Signor Baldeschi," he insisted almost beseechingly, with the respectful, as it were heartbroken, moderation of a social inferior who knows he is in the right, "how could I have possibly cut you if you hadn't moved? Believe me, you *did* move . . . but it's nothing much—just wait a moment." He went to the table, uncorked a little bottle, took a piece of cotton-wool from a packet and soaked it in the spirit.

Beside myself with rage, I shouted: "What d'you mean, it's nothing much? . . . it's a very bad cut"; and, snatching the cotton-wool out of his hand, I went over to the mirror. The burning sensation of the spirit gave the final touch to my exasperation. "So it's nothing much, eh?" I shouted, throwing away the blood-stained cotton-wool in a fresh access of fury. "You don't know what you're talking about, Antonio . . . and look here—you'd better clear out."

"But, Signor Baldeschi . . . I haven't finished shaving you . . ."

"That doesn't matter. . . . Clear out and don't show yourself here again," I cried. "I don't want to see you here again—d'you understand?"

"But, Signor Baldeschi . . ."

"That's enough . . . go away and don't let me see you again . . . never again . . . get out—d'you understand?"

"Am I to come to-morrow?"

"No—not to-morrow nor any other day. . . . That's enough, I tell you." I stood shouting in the middle of the room, the towel still tied round my neck. Then I saw him make a slight bow—an ironical bow, I dare say—murmuring "As you wish"; then he went to the door and disappeared.

Once I was alone, my anger gradually calmed down. I took off the towel, wiped away the small amount of soap that remained on my face and looked at myself in the mirror. Antonio's cut had been inflicted at the moment when he had almost finished shaving me, so that my face, apart from the long red wound, was smooth. I soaked another piece of cotton-wool in spirit and disinfected the cut thoroughly. I was thinking, in the meantime, about the strange impulse that had driven me to dismiss Antonio, and I realized that the cut had been merely a pretext. I had in truth been wanting to dismiss him all the time; and at the first opportunity I had done so. But it did not escape me that I had dismissed him only when his dismissal no longer harmed me— that is, after I had finished my story. I was aware that, in consequence, I could not represent the barber's dismissal to Leda as a homage to her wishes; for, just as I had kept Antonio, in spite of her accusations, for selfish reasons, so now, for similar reasons, I had got rid of him. At this thought I was conscious of a certain remorse; and for the first time I understood that, perhaps without realizing it, I had not behaved well towards my wife. Meanwhile I was dressing and, when I was ready, I went downstairs.

She was already in the dining-room, sitting at the table. We ate in silence for some time, and then I said: "You know, I've sacked Antonio . . . really and truly."

Without raising her eyes from her plate, she asked: "And what will you do about shaving?"

"I shall try and shave myself," I answered; "anyhow it's only for a few days, because we shall be leaving here, shan't we? . . . I don't know what came over him to-day, he gave me a cut as long as my finger . . . look."

She raised her eyes and scrutinized the wound. Then, apprehensively, she asked: "You put some antiseptic on it?"

"Yes . . . And I must tell you that the cut was only an excuse . . . actually I couldn't bear Antonio any longer. . . . You were quite right."

"What do you mean by that?"

I saw that I could not produce Angelo's information without deferring the time when I had received it. And so I lied: "This morning I talked to Angelo about Antonio . . . I discovered that he's an unbridled libertine . . . it seems he's extremely well known as such throughout the whole district . . . he annoys all the women. So I thought that maybe you were right . . . although there's still no proof that in your case he acted with intention . . . and I took advantage of the cut to get rid of him."

She said nothing. I went on: "It's odd, all the same. You'd never think . . . really I don't know what women can see in him—bald, yellow, short, fat. . . . He's not exactly an Adonis."

"Did you find your paper in the town?" she asked.

"Not exactly . . . but I got some foolscap paper— that'll do." I saw that the subject of Antonio was displeasing to her and willingly changed the conversation, following her lead. "I shall begin the typing to-day," I said. "I want to do it in the afternoons and evenings as well. . . . I shall get it done quicker like that."

She was silent and went on eating in a composed

manner. I talked a little more about my book and about my plans, and then said: "I'm going to dedicate this book to you, because without your love I should never have written it"; and I took her hand. She raised her eyes and smiled at me. This time, the goodwill of which I seemed to catch a glimpse every now and then in her attitude towards me was so obvious that even a blind man would have noticed it. I was struck dumb, and sat holding her hand, my enthusiasm chilled. She was smiling at me just as a mother smiles at a small child which, at a moment when she does not want to be bothered with it, runs up to her panting and says: "Mummy, when I'm big I want to be a general." Then she said: "And what will the dedication be?"

Mentally I translated this into: "And which branch of the army d'you want to be in?" I answered, rather embarrassed: "Oh, something very simple . . . for instance, *To Leda* . . . or, *To my wife* . . . Why? Would you like a longer dedication?"

"Oh no, I didn't mean anything."

Her attention was certainly elsewhere. And I, withdrawing my hand, fell into an absorbed silence, gazing through the window at the trees outside. I was thinking that one or other of us ought to break this silence, but nothing happened. Her silence, one would have said, was decisive and final; she seemed shut up in her own thoughts and in no way desirous of coming out of them. In order not to show my disappointment, I tried to joke, and said: "D'you know what dedication a certain writer once made to his wife? *To my wife, without whose absence this book could never have been written.*"

She gave a faint smile and I added hastily: "But of course our case is just exactly the opposite. . . . I could never have written it without your *presence*."

This time she did not even smile. I could not restrain myself any longer, and said: "Well, if you don't want it, we won't put any dedication at all."

Some bitterness must have been discernible in my voice, for she seemed to recollect herself with an effort and, taking my hand again, she replied: "Oh, Silvio, how can you imagine that I don't want it?" But this time again the goodwill was too obvious; it was just like that of a mother whose child, discouraged, says: "Well then, if you don't want me to, I won't be a general," and she answers: "Oh, but I do want you to be one . . . and I want you to win lots of battles." I saw that this conversation was profitless, and I was seized again by the same irritation that I had felt with Antonio and which I had then attributed to hunger. I rose brusquely, saying: "I think Anna's already taken the coffee outside."

12

LATER, when she left me to rest, I went up to my study to begin my typing. I arranged my typewriter on the desk, opened it and put the cover down on the floor. On the right of the machine I placed my manuscript, on the left the blank sheets and the carbon paper. I took three sheets of paper, inserted two sheets of copying paper between them, put them into the machine and tapped out the title. But I had not arranged the paper rightly, and the title, as I at once saw, was all to one side; besides, I had forgotten to type it in capital letters. I took out the three sheets and inserted three more. This time the title came out right in the middle, but on examination I found that I had put the carbon paper in upside down, so that the two copies were spoiled.

Irritated, I tore the sheets out of the machine and put in others; this time I made two or three mistakes which made the title incomprehensible. All of a sudden a feeling almost of fear came over me. I rose from the desk and started wandering round the room looking at the old German prints that adorned the walls—"The Castle of Kammersee", "Panorama of the Town of Weimar", "Storm over Lake Starnberg", "The Falls of the Rhine". The house was plunged in a profound silence, the shutters were half closed, and the dim light inside the room invited one to sleep. I reflected that I was tired, that the present conditions were not suitable for me to embark upon my task of copying; so I went and lay down on a very hard sofa, in the darkest corner of the room.

I stretched out my hand towards a little table laden with knick-knacks that stood beside the sofa, and took up a red leather, gilt-edged memorandum book: it was an old "keepsake" of 1860. Its former owner had made, on each page, a pen-and-ink drawing of a little landscape —very similar, in their homely style, to the prints I had just been looking at. Beneath each landscape, in a cursive "English" calligraphy, were reflections and maxims in French. I looked at the landscapes one by one and read through many of these extremely sentimental and conventional reflections. Meanwhile drowsiness was coming over me. I put the book back on the table and dropped off to sleep.

I slept for perhaps an hour. In my sleep I seemed, every now and then, to wake up, and I could see the desk, the chair, the typewriter, and thought I ought to be working, and was conscious of a bitter feeling of impotence. Finally, as though at a signal, I awoke completely and leapt to my feet.

The room was plunged in gloom. I went to the window, threw open the shutters; the sky was still luminous, but the sun was low and came in slantingly through the window. Without thinking of anything I sat down at the desk and started typing.

I tapped out a couple of pages mechanically and then, at the third, broke off and fell into deep meditation. Actually I was not thinking at all; merely I could not get the sense of the words that I had written with such ardour a few days before. I saw that they were words, but they remained mere words and it seemed to me that they had no weight, no meaning. They were parts of speech, not objects, parts of speech such as are drawn up in rows on the pages of dictionaries, parts of speech and nothing more. At that moment my wife appeared in the doorway, asking whether I wanted to have tea. I welcomed this proposal with relief, glad of some distraction from the feeling of remoteness and absurdity that I experienced in front of my manuscript; and I followed her downstairs. She was already dressed for our customary walk, and tea was on the table. I pulled myself together with an effort and began chatting in a self-possessed manner as I drank my tea. My wife now appeared less abstracted and preoccupied, and this pleased me. After tea we went out and strolled down the drive towards the gate.

As I have already said, there were few walks in that neighbourhood: and so we turned off down a lane that we knew extremely well, through the fields. I walked in front and Leda followed me. My mind, as I soon realized, was still bogged in that sensation of vagueness and lack of comprehension that my manuscript had aroused in me, but I made an effort—with, to tell the truth, only partial success—to thrust away this preoccupation and to talk lightly of unimportant matters. The lane wound about amongst the fields, according to the lay-out of the various farms, linking the groups of farm buildings together. Sometimes it would coincide with a threshing-floor, in front of an isolated cottage; and then it would start twisting about again between two hedges or along a ditch beside a vegetable garden or by the last row of vines at the edge of a vineyard. In the clear, even, brilliant autumn light the entire plain was visible, as far as the eye could reach—every field, every patch of cultivation—flat, luminous, with a few trees here and there, dark against their background of clear sky but with every leaf lit up in the sunshine. When we came to a little hump-backed bridge spanning a deep ditch I stopped to look at the view and my wife went on in front. I remember that she was wearing a coat and skirt of grey cloth flecked with red, green, yellow and blue. When I first glanced after her as she walked ahead I was frightened, because it suddenly seemed to me that she too, like the words of my manuscript, was nothing more than a speck in space. I said, gently: "Leda", and felt I was saying the most absurd thing in the world. I went on: "My name is Silvio Baldeschi and I married a woman whose name is Leda"; and I felt I had not said anything at all. It came into my mind, all of a sudden, that the only way I could escape from this atmosphere of unreality was by receiving or inflicting pain—for instance by seizing my wife by the hair, throwing her down on the sharp stones of the path, and receiving from her, in turn, a good kick on the shins. In the same way, perhaps I should awaken to the value of my manuscript by tearing it up and throwing it into the fire.

These reflections brought me a vivid feeling that I must be mad: was it not then possible to lay hold of one's own, or other people's, existence except through the medium of pain? But I consoled myself slightly with the thought that if it were so, if not only what I had written but also my wife, whom I knew I loved, seemed to me incomprehensible, then this feeling of absurdity did not depend upon the quality of what I had written but upon myself.

My wife was looking for a place to sit down—a difficult matter in a countryside like that, where every foot of space was cultivated, every plant had its use, and every clod of earth held a seed. We came at last to a cleft in the ground at the bottom of which ran a little stream called—perhaps because of its twisting course—the Ess. At this point the grassy banks sloped gently down, and the stream formed a tiny pool, like a round mirror of dense green water, overshadowed by three or four poplar-trees. A sloping strip of cement, half in and half out of the water, such as is used by women for beating and wringing out clothes, showed that this apparently remote spot was used as a washing-place. But in any case, as Leda said, throwing herself down on the grass, in this part of the country every little corner is put to some use and there is nothing to be done about it.

We started talking quietly, in that moment just before sunset when both light and sound are softened. My wife had picked a blade of grass and was chewing it; and I, sitting a little lower down the bank, was looking at the vague shadows of the poplars reflected in the glassy water of the stream. We spoke for a little about the day and the place, and then, on a very slight pretext (I had asked her if she would like to go up into the mountains in the winter) she started relating an episode in her past life which had, in fact, occurred in a mountain resort two years before. My wife's first marriage, as I have already explained, lasted only a very short time, and after that, for ten years, she had lived alone and had had, as I was aware, numerous lovers. I had no feelings of jealousy for these predecessors of mine, and she, seeing that I was indifferent, had taken to talking about them, circumspectly at first and then quite openly. Why she should have done so, I do not know: perhaps out of vanity, or— in her present very different circumstances— from a vestige of regret for the uncontrolled freedom she had enjoyed. I cannot say that these stories gave me any pleasure; when I least expected it, I would feel myself giving a start of surprise, the involuntary effect, as it were, of a sensibility I did not know I possessed. Certainly this was not jealousy; nor, however, was it the complete, rational objectivity that I prided myself on being able to display. But when, that day, chewing her blade of grass, her eyes staring fixedly not at me but at something which she perhaps saw in imagination, she told me the story of one of her adventures, I was aware that the slightly uncomfortable feeling that her reminiscences usually aroused in me was, this time, proving agreeable, like a fortifying tonic to someone who is feeling faint. When I sat down I had been a prey to a distressing sense of unreality; and now that warm, sensual voice of hers was speaking to me of real things, of things which had really happened and which, into the bargain, had happened to her and were displeasing to me. In others, more hot-blooded, these memories might perhaps have kindled a raging hatred; but to me, bloodless as I was, they restored the sense of what I myself was and of what she was to me. Certainly I suffered when I listened to her telling me, quite plainly, how she had allowed herself to be approached by a man she liked, how she had let herself be kissed, how they had slept together; but this suffering, just sufficing, as it did, to re-awaken my failing vitality, became almost pleasant and lost its harmful and gratuitous quality. It was a poison, perhaps, but one of those poisons which, taken in small doses, restore the patient to life.

She was telling me of an adventure that she had had with a red-haired lieutenant in the Alpini. "I was in the mountains in March," she said, "and since the snow had already gone, where I was, I went up and stayed in a climbers' hostel at about 5,000 feet. Nobody ever came there, and I spent the days on the terrace in front of the hostel, in a long chair, reading and basking in the sun. One day a group of Alpini came up from the valley. I was on the terrace, as usual, and they started taking off their skis all round about me, so as to go in and have a drink in the hostel. Amongst them was a young officer, with red hair and a freckled face and blue eyes. He wore no hat or jacket—just a grey-green shirt—and as he stooped down to undo his skis I saw that his back was youthful and vigorous—powerful, but slim at the waist. When he stood up again he looked at me and I at him, and that was enough for me. A great fear came over me that he hadn't understood—whereas really he had understood perfectly well, as you shall see. I remember that I got up and, all upset, I went into the main room of the hostel. He went and stuck his skis upright in the snow and then came in after me. His companions had already sat down at a table and he sat down with them, with his back to the window and his face to the room. I went to the counter and ordered tea, then took a table opposite theirs. They were laughing and joking, and I, like a fool, was trying to catch his eye. Afterwards he told me that he had observed my manœuvre; but at the moment, seeing that he did not even deign to glance at me, I thought he had not noticed. At last he looked at me, and then, so that there should be no possible mistake, I put my fingers to my lips and threw him a kiss, like a little girl. He saw me do this but gave no sign of having understood; and then I began to be afraid that he didn't like me. As if I had been too hot, I took off my jacket, and, pretending that I wanted to pull up my shoulder-strap under my blouse, I uncovered my shoulder slightly. But next moment I felt angry, and I left the room and went back to my long chair on the terrace. They sat a little longer over their drinks and then they too came out, took their skis and went off. I sat waiting in my chair, still uncertain. The sun went down and still I waited, numb with cold and now almost without hope. I was completely in despair when he suddenly appeared coming down the slope on his skis. I went forward to meet him, filled with joy, and he said: 'I had to invent a whole lot of excuses . . . they didn't believe me, but that really doesn't matter.' That was what he said, just as though we had always known each other. I didn't answer; I was so excited I hadn't even the strength to speak. He took off his skis very slowly, and I took him by the hand and led him straight to my room upstairs. Fancy! I never knew what his name was!"

I have written down this story in her own brief, laconic words. She never dallied over the sensual part of these recitals of hers; but she appeared to suggest it by the rich tones of her voice and by a kind of lively, carnal participation of her whole body in what she was saying. She became animated; her beauty was intensified. And that day, when she had finished, I seemed to understand that there was, in her, a vitality stronger than any moral rule; and that I myself had a need to draw upon this vitality if—as, indeed, was the case—it was necessary for me to repress certain reactions of my own sensibility. For a moment I had not, in fact, been a husband listening, with mind disturbed, to the love reminiscences of his wife, but rather a dry clod of earth saved from crumbling into dust by the timely fall of a beneficent shower of rain. I looked at her as she sat there, absorbed in thought, chewing her blade of grass, and I realized, to my surprise, that I was no longer conscious of that painful feeling of unreality.

13

WE went slowly back to the house, and I was calm and happy again as at my best moments, and I talked and joked with full self-confidence. When we reached the house it was later than usual, and my wife went straight upstairs to her room to change for dinner. I put a record on the radiogramophone—a Mozart quartet—and sat down in the armchair. I felt myself to be in a joyful, detached state of mind. Soon, when the quartet reached the minuet and entered upon the ceremonious but touching dialogue of this dance, with its loud, sonorous questionings and its melancholy but graceful replies, the thought came to me that there was more in these questions and answers than a mere masculine and feminine tone of voice: there were two well-defined attitudes, one active, the other passive, one aggressive, the other shy, one flattered, the other flattering. The notes, I thought, suggested a relationship that was unchangeable through time, and little did it matter whether the two people who met in the dance belonged to to-day or to two centuries ago. It might be we two, my wife and I; and this was the dance that we danced in our own way, as, before us, in all ages, innumerable couples had danced it. Lost in my thoughts, I did not notice the passing of time, and was almost astonished when I saw Leda appear in front of me, in the white, low-cut dress of the evening before. She stopped the gramophone halfway through the record, saying with a slight air of impatience: "I don't know why, but I don't want to listen to any music this evening." Then, sitting down beside me, on the arm of my chair, she asked me in a casual tone of voice: "So you're going to begin typing your story this evening?"

As she asked this question, she looked at herself in the mirror from her handbag and re-adjusted the bunch of fresh flowers in her hair. I answered with satisfaction: "Yes, this evening I shall begin the typing and I shall work at least until midnight. . . . I want to get on with it and finish it within a few days."

Touching her hair, she said: "Until midnight? Won't you be sleepy?"

"Why?" I replied. "I'm used to working at night. . . . I want," I concluded, putting my arm round her waist, "I want to finish quickly so as to be able to devote myself completely to you."

She put the mirror back in her bag and asked: "Why? Don't you think we're enough together as it is?"

I answered, in a meaning tone of voice: "No, not in the way I want."

"Ah, I understand," she said. And, rising from the armchair, she started walking up and down the room in an impatient, tireless sort of way, "What's the matter?" I asked.

"I'm hungry," she replied, in a hard, irritated tone of voice; "that's what's the matter." She added, more gently: "Aren't you hungry too?"

"So-so," I answered, "but I don't want to eat too much, or I shall be sleepy later on."

"You certainly take good care of yourself," she said;

and I gave a start, for it was an unpleasant remark and I was not prepared for it.

"What d'you mean by that?" I asked quietly.

She saw that she had offended me, and, stopping in front of me, touched me caressingly, saying: "I'm sorry . . . when one's hungry one becomes aggressive. . . . Don't take any notice of me."

"It's quite true," I said, remembering the incident with Antonio; "hunger makes one irritable."

"Well, well," she went on hastily, "how d'you like this frock?"

Possibly she asked me this in order to change the conversation; for, as I have said, it was the same dress that she had worn the evening before and I had already seen it several times. Nevertheless I said, indulgently: "Yes, it's lovely, and it suits you very well. . . . Turn round and let me look."

She revolved obediently, so as to show herself; and then I noticed a small alteration. The evening before I had remarked that, round her belly and hips, beneath the light, almost transparent material of the dress, she wore an elastic belt, of American type, made of silk and rubber, that she sometimes put on to preserve the correct line of her figure. I did not at all like this belt, which, besides being visible, was so hard and tight underneath the loose-fitting dress that, to the touch, it was unpleasantly suggestive of some orthopædic apparatus. But now, as I immediately noticed, the belt was not there; and she did in fact look more supple and slightly fatter. "You haven't put on your American armour-plating this evening," I said casually.

She glanced at me and then answered with indifference: "I didn't put it on because I was bored with it. . . . But how did you know?"

"Because yesterday you had it on, and it was obvious."

She said nothing, and just at that moment the maid came to tell us that dinner was ready. We went into the dining-room and sat down, and my wife helped herself. I noticed then that, contrary to what she had said before, she was clearly not hungry: she had taken only half a spoonful from the dish that was offered to her. I remarked as I helped myself: "You were so hungry . . . and now you won't touch anything."

She gave me a look of displeasure, as though she were irritated at my having caught her in a contradiction. "I was wrong," she said. "I'm not really in the least hungry. . . . In fact the sight of food makes me feel rather sick."

"Don't you feel well?" I asked anxiously.

She hesitated, then answered all in one breath, in a very low voice: "I think I'm all right . . . but I'm not hungry." I noticed that her voice was languid, and her breath seemed almost to fail her between one syllable and the next. Then she was silent, poking about with her fork in her plate; then she put down the fork and sighed deeply, laying her hand on her breast. "But you *don't* feel well," I said, alarmed.

This time she admitted it. "No . . . I feel rather oppressed," she said in an exhausted voice, as though she were going to faint.

"Would you like to lie down on the divan?"

"No."

"Would you like me to call the maid?"

"No . . . but you can give me something to drink."

I poured her out some wine, and she drank it and it appeared to revive her. The maid brought in the fruit and she did not touch it; I ate a bunch of grapes, slowly, while she looked at me with eyes that seemed to be counting each single grape as I raised it to my mouth. The moment the stripped stalk fell from my hand, she jumped impetuously to her feet, saying: "Now I'm going to bed."

"Don't you want any coffee?" I asked, alarmed at her loud, distressed tone of voice, as I followed her into the drawing-room.

"No, no coffee, I want to sleep." She was standing at the door as she spoke, stiff, impatient, her fingers on the handle.

I told the maid to bring my coffee to the study upstairs and followed my wife, who had already opened the door and was making for the staircase. I joined her and said, in a casual way: "Now I shall start work."

"And I shall sleep," she answered, without turning round.

"Are you sure you haven't a temperature?" I asked, reaching out to place my hand on her forehead. She dodged away and said, impatiently: "Oh, Silvio, with you it's always necessary to dot the i's and cross the t's . . . I'm not well—and that's all there is to it."

I was silent, feeling slightly embarrassed. When we reached the landing, I took her hand as though to kiss it, hesitated, and then said: "I want to ask you a favour."

"What favour?" she asked, with a break in her voice which surprised me.

"I want you to come in here a moment," I said awkwardly, "and leave a kiss on the first page of my story. . . . It'll bring me luck."

She gave a laugh which was at the same time affectionate and forced; but both the affection and the effort seemed to me to be oddly sincere. And she went hastily into my study, exclaiming: "How superstitious you are! . . . How silly you are! . . . But just as you like. . . ."

I turned on the light, but she had already found her way in the darkness to my desk. "Which is the page? . . . Tell me which page it is I've got to kiss," she kept repeating with a sort of feverish enthusiasm.

I went up to her and handed her the first page, on which I had typed nothing but the title: *Conjugal Love*. She seized hold of it, read out the title aloud, commenting upon it with a grimace which I could not understand, then raised the sheet of paper to her mouth and pressed her lips against it. "Now are you content?" she said.

Just beneath the title, the page now bore the mark of her lips—two red semicircles, like two flower-petals. I looked at it for some time, with a feeling of satisfaction, and then I said softly: "Thank you, my dear."

She raised her hand and quickly stroked my cheek, then moved towards the door, saying hurriedly: "Good luck with your work, then . . . I'm going to go and sleep. . . . I really feel very tired. . . . Please don't knock at my door for any reason whatsoever. . . . I just want to sleep— that's all. . . . Till to-morrow, then. . . ."

"Very well . . . till to-morrow."

She went out, almost running into the maid who was bringing in the coffee. When she too had gone, I lit a cigarette, sat down at my desk, drank two cups of coffee straight off, and finally took the cover off the typewriter. I was conscious of an extraordinary mental lucidity, as though, instead of the usual confused, unwieldy tangle of vague and contradictory thoughts, my head contained a clean, precise, perfectly adjusted mechanism like that of a weighing-machine or a clock. I felt that this mechanism excluded all vanity, pride, fear and ambition. It was the precision instrument, incorruptible, impersonal, by means of which I was preparing to gauge, to appraise, to perfect my work as I copied it out. A cigarette between my lips, my eyes fixed on my sheet of paper, I started typing, continuing the page which was already half done.

I typed, perhaps, four lines, and then I put down my cigarette in the ashtray, pushed the typewriter to one side, took up the manuscript and began to read it. As I have said, I was feeling exceptionally clear in the head; and now, as I typed the first four lines, I had become conscious of a feeling of falsity which was quite distinct and exactly like the dull sound of a cracked glass. In other words, it had flashed across my mind that the story not merely was not the masterpiece that I had imagined, but was actually bad. As I have already mentioned, I have a certain literary experience and, in given circumstances, am also capable of being a tolerable critic. I realized at that moment that, with my present extraordinary, and aggressive, mental lucidity, my whole critical faculty was brought into play, to an amazing degree, upon the page

I held in my hand. The words were no longer mere words but fragments of a metal that I was gradually testing, with perfect certainty, by means of the touchstone of my own taste. I did not read it straight through because I did not wish to be caught up in the rhythm of the narrative; but I read pieces here and there, and the more I read the more disquieted I became. It seemed to me impossible that I was making a mistake now: the story was thoroughly bad, beyond any remedy. All of a sudden, seized by an almost scientific craze for objectivity, I took a sheet of blank paper, grasped my fountain pen and started jotting down my observations as they came into my mind, just as I did when I had a book to review.

At the top of the page I wrote, in a firm hand: "Remarks upon the story *Conjugal Love*, by Silvio Baldeschi"; then I drew a line under it and began to make notes. I followed the method I usually adopted in composing my critical articles—that is, analysing the work disconnectedly in all its various aspects and then finally fusing all these detailed observations into one single, comprehensive verdict. Of course I had no intention of writing an article about myself; I merely wished to establish, to a certain extent, the reasons for that first feeling that the story was bad. Also, perhaps, to punish myself for having believed it a masterpiece. But, above all, to reach some clear and final conclusion about my own literary ambitions.

14

THIS is what I wrote on my new page. *First:* style. And then, underneath, quickly: polished, correct, decorous, but never original, never personal, never fresh. Full of vague generalizations, discursive where it should be brief, brief where it should be discursive, in effect entirely redundant because entirely the result of application. A style without character, the style of a diligent composition in which there is not the slightest trace of poetical feeling. *Second:* plasticity. None. States things instead of representing them, writes them instead of portraying them. Lack of evident truth, of volume, of solidity. *Third:* characters. Negative. One feels they were not created by sympathetic intuition but studiously copied and transcribed from nature through the instrumentality—in any case defective—of a judgment that was indecisive, clouded and elementary. They are mosaics of minute but lifeless observations, not living, free creations. They disintegrate, they contradict themselves, they disappear, at moments, from the page, leaving only their names behind; and these names—whether the characters are called Paolo or Lorenzo or Elisa or Maria—betray their unreality because one feels that they could be changed without doing any harm. They are not characters at all, in fact, but photographs out of focus. *Fourth:* psychological truth. Poor. Too much casuistry, too many subtleties, too many irrelevant remarks, and too little common sense. "Psychologism", not psychology.

One feels that the author moves from outside to inside, at random, not by the main road of truth but along the byways of sophistry. *Fifth:* feeling. Cold and withered, beneath swellings and outbursts and flights which betray its real emptiness and feebleness. Sentimentality, not feeling. *Sixth:* plot. Ill-constructed, unbalanced, full of incongruities, of subterfuges and padding and other dishonest tricks beneath its apparent efficiency and smoothness. Plenty of *deus ex machina* and interventions on the part of the author. Movement is confined to the periphery, and is mechanical, for at the centre there is no motive power. *Seventh and last:* comprehensive verdict. The book of a dilettante, of a person who, though endowed with intelligence, culture and taste, is completely lacking in creative powers. The book fails to reveal anything fresh, or any fresh turn of sensibility. It is a book founded upon other books, it is second or third rate in quality, it is a hot-house product. *Practical conclusion:* can it be published? Yes, of course, it can certainly be published—why not in an *édition de luxe*, with one or two lithographs by some good artist? And, after a suitable propaganda drive in literary circles, it could also have what is commonly called a *succès d'estime*, that is, a number of reviews that are eulogistic, even enthusiastic, according to whether it is worth the reviewers' while and according to their degree of friendliness towards the author. *But the book itself does not count.* I underlined this last sentence which summed up everything that I thought about my story, considered for a moment, and then added the following postscript: the fact remains, however, that the book was written in a state of mind of the most perfect and enthusiastic happiness and that it is certainly the best that can be expected from the author. Indeed the latter, while he was writing it, was convinced that he had created a masterpiece. It follows from this that the author expressed himself in the book as he really is—a man lacking in creative feeling, a mere day-dreamer, well-intentioned, sterile. This book is the faithful mirror of such a man.

That was all for the moment. I put the manuscript back in its folder, took the sheets of paper out of the typewriter and put its cover on. Then I got up, lit a cigarette and started walking up and down the room. It dawned upon me then that the mental clear-sightedness, with which I had before been so pleased, had now transformed itself into the false lucidity of a feverish, desperate delirium. After having made me write that severe judgment upon my own work, this lucidity still persisted in my mind, as moonlight persists on the surface of a stormy sea where float the fragments, great and small, of a shipwreck. My mind circled lucidly, feverishly, round the final wreck of my ambitions, illuminating it in all its aspects and rendering it all the more bitter and complete. In those twenty days during which I had done nothing but write, closing my mind against all other preoccupations, an enormous mass of discouragement seemed to have accumulated in the depth of my consciousness. Now the dykes of my crazy presumption had burst and it came flooding out in every direction; and I, though so lucid, felt myself overwhelmed. I threw away the cigarette I had only just lit and, almost without knowing what I did, raised my hands and pressed them against my temples.

I realized that the failure of my book foreshadowed the far wider failure of my whole life, and I felt that my whole being rebelled against this result. It is impossible to describe what I felt—the acute sense of a sudden crumbling to pieces, of a headlong plunge into absurdity and emptiness. Above all, I rebelled against the picture of myself provided by my book. I did not want to be a trifler, an incompetent, a weakling. And yet I knew that, just because I rebelled against it, this picture was a true one.

In this fury of despair I felt as if my body no longer had any weight and as if I were flying about the room, like a dry, dead leaf swept along by a violent wind. Not only was I no longer aware of the movements I made, but even of the thoughts that formed themselves in my brain. No doubt the idea of appealing to my wife in this distress, with the object of finding not so much consolation as a straw to seize hold of in the flood that overwhelmed me, flashed into my mind before I translated it into action. But it is certain that I became conscious of it when, without realizing it, I had already opened the study door, had crossed the landing and found myself in front of her door. I raised my hand and knocked. I noticed at the same moment that the door was not shut but merely ajar, and I was struck—I do not know why—by the precautionary appearance that it had in that position. There was no answer to my two knocks, so I knocked again, louder, and then, after waiting a reasonable time, pushed the door open and went in.

The room was dark, so I turned on the central light, and the first thing I saw, in that pale illumination, was my wife's nightdress laid out, the sleeves outspread, on the untouched bed. I thought she must have been unable to sleep and had gone down into the garden; but at the same time I could not help feeling a certain annoyance: she could have knocked and told me—why should she have gone alone? I glanced at the alarm clock on the bed-table and was astonished to see that about three hours had passed since I had made my wife kiss the title-page of my story. Events had followed so thick and fast upon each other that it had seemed to me to be scarcely half an hour. I left the room and went on down the staircase.

The blue and red glass door of the drawing-room was lit up, and the whole house appeared to be awake. I went into the room, sure that I should find my wife there, but it was deserted. The book that she was reading was on the table, open and upside down, as though she had put it down in the midst of her reading. Beside the book was an ashtray full of long cigarette-ends, all stained with lipstick. My wife had obviously come downstairs again shortly after saying good-night to me and had spent the evening in the drawing-room, smoking and reading. Then she must have gone out for a walk in the garden; but not long before, since the air was still filled with smoke in spite of the french window being wide open. Perhaps she had only just that moment gone out and I could catch her up. So I, in my turn, went out on to the open space in front of the house.

The white gleam of the moonlight on the gravel reminded me of our walk the night before to the farm buildings; and all of a sudden, in my state of combined despair and exaltation, I was overcome with the desire to do, now, that thing which it had not been possible for me to do then. I would make love to Leda on the threshing-floor, by the light of that magnificent full moon, in the silence of the sleeping countryside, with all the passion that came to me from the sense of my own impotence. It was certainly a very natural, very logical, very ordinary impulse that suggested this plan to me; but this time I was content to let myself go, both in feeling and action, like a peasant who seeks, in the docile embrace of his wife, comfort and a sort of compensation for damage done by a hailstorm. After all, nothing remained to me, in the wreck of my ambition, but to accept my status as a human being, similar in all respects to that of other men. After that night I would be content to be just a decent fellow with some knowledge of letters and modestly conscious of his own limitations, but at the same time the lover, and the beloved, of a young and beautiful wife. It would be upon her that I would exercise my unfortunate passion for poetry. I would live this amorous experience of mine poetically, seeing that I could not write about it. Women love these unsuccessful men who have renounced all ambitions except that of making them happy.

Thinking thus, I had started down the drive, deeply absorbed as I walked, and with head bowed. Then I raised my eyes and saw Leda. Or rather, I caught a glimpse of her just for one moment, a long way away, as she rounded the curve of the drive and disappeared. A ray of moonlight lay across the road at that point. For one instant I saw distinctly her white dress, her bare neck and the fair gold of her hair. Then she vanished, and I was convinced that she was going towards the farm buildings. It pleased me to think that she was making her way to the threshing-floor, to the place where I wanted to make love to her, just as though she were going to keep an appointment and yet without knowing that the appointment was with me. I too rounded the curve, and then I saw her again as she turned into a side lane which, as I knew, led into the path that ran between the fields and the park. I almost called out to her but checked myself, thinking that I would catch up with her and throw my arms round her, taking her by surprise.

I was in the lane when she turned into the path; and when I started along the path, she was already walking along the bottom of the knoll on which the farm buildings stood. She was almost running, and for the first time her white face, as it passed quickly through the black shadows of the trees, gave me a feeling of strangeness. When I in turn arrived below the farm buildings I stopped, struck by some presentiment that I could not explain. I could see her now climbing up the steep slope towards the threshing-floor, where stood the round masses of the straw-stacks. Bending forwards, she clutched at the bushes as she slipped and stumbled, and in her strained, eager face with its staring eyes, in the movement of her whole body, I was once more conscious of her resemblance to a goat, climbing a slope in search of food. Soon, when she reached the top, the figure of a man appeared out of the shadow, bent down and, taking her by the arm, pulled her up almost bodily. Twisting round in order to steady her, the man turned and I recognized Antonio.

Now I understood everything. A great coldness came over me, and at the same time an utter astonishment that I had not understood before—not just a short time before, when I had gone into her room and found it empty, but three weeks ago, when she had asked me to dismiss the barber. This wondering astonishment was mingled with a cruel distress which took my breath away and lay heavy on my heart. I wanted not to look, if only out of self-respect; instead of which I stared greedily, with straining eyes. The threshing-floor was like a stage high above me, lit by the moon. When Leda was standing upright again, I saw the man seize her by the arms, seeking to pull her towards him, and she, twisting and pulling herself back, was trying to resist. The moonlight fell on her face, and then I saw that it was distorted into that mute, tense grimace that I had noticed on other occasions; her mouth was half open in a grin that displayed both disgust and desire, her eyes were dilated and her chin thrust out. Meanwhile her whole body, with its violent writhings that suggested some kind of dance, seemed a continuation of her facial distortion.

Antonio was trying to draw her to him and she was resisting him and pulling away from him. Then—I do not know how—she turned her back on him, he seized her by the elbows and she started twisting and writhing again with her back against him, throwing herself back into his arms and yet all the time refusing him her mouth. I noticed that, in these spasmodic contortions of hers, she raised herself up on the tips of her toes; and again the idea of a dance came to me. For a short time they continued struggling together in this way, one behind the other, and then, changing position—as though in some new kind of minuet—there they were, side by side. Her arm was thrown across his chest, his arms were round her waist and her head was flung back. Then they slipped back, one against the other, and were face to face again. This time she drew back her head and her breast as he held her in his arms, and at the same moment lifted her dress, uncovering her legs and her belly. For the first time I realized that those legs were the legs of a dancer—white, muscular, slim, with feet extended and supported on the tips of the toes. She threw back the upper part of her body and thrust forward her belly against his, while he stood still and tried to make her stand straight so that he could embrace her. The moonlight shone upon the pair, and it looked now as though they were really performing some kind of dance, he erect and motionless, she circling about him: a dance without music and without rules but none the less obedient to a frantic rhythm of its own. Finally she caused him to lose his balance, or he did so deliberately; and they fell back together, disappearing into the shadow of one of the stacks.

15

I WAS almost sorry to see them disappear. The moon, between the two straw-stacks in shadow, was shining brilliantly on the empty threshing-floor, upon the spot where I had seen them pressed together in their dance, and for a moment I thought that it had not been my wife and the barber whom I had seen, but two nocturnal spirits conjured up by the splendour of the moonlight. I was overwhelmed by what I had witnessed, but I made a great effort to control myself and to take a detached view of it; in this my æsthetic sense came to my rescue, and for the first time I felt that it was being put to a supreme test. I remembered that, on the previous night, the moonlight on the threshing-floor had suggested to me the idea of a panic love, in the mild, silent night; and I saw that my thought and my desire had been right. Only, at the last moment, someone else had taken my place. I had divined, instinctively, the beauty of that embrace; but the embrace had taken place without me.

There flashed upon me, however, a sudden suspicion that this effort to be objective was merely a device on the part of wounded pride; and I said to myself that I could reason and understand as much as I liked, but the fact remained: I had been cruelly deceived, my wife had betrayed me with a barber, and this betrayal stood between me and my wife. At this thought I felt a sharp pain; and I realized that, for the first time since I had seen Leda in Antonio's arms, I was assuming the role that had been forced upon me—that of the husband of an unfaithful wife. But at the same time I knew that I was neither willing nor able to accept that position. I had not hitherto been a husband like other husbands; our relations had been just as I had wished them to be and not as our married state might have prescribed; and so they must remain. I must continue to be reasonable and, above all, understanding. This was my vocation, and not even betrayal could justify my abandoning it. Even as I ran back towards the villa, I started feverishly reconstructing in my mind the exact course events had taken between myself, my wife and Antonio.

The man, it was certain, was a libertine, but it was possible that at the beginning there had been no deliberate intention on his part, and that the first contact with my wife had been merely accidental. In the same way she had been truly and sincerely indignant at what she had called "want of respect" on the part of the barber—although the excess of this indignation concealed, even at that time, the beginnings of an unconscious excitement and attraction. Actually, in asking me to dismiss the barber, she had asked me to defend her, not so much against the barber as against herself; but I had not understood and, selfishly, had thought of nothing but my own immediate convenience. She had not discerned the selfishness in my behaviour, just as she had not understood the deeper motives of her own, and she had resigned herself, as she usually did, out of affection and goodwill. She had thus endured a situation in which the man who had insulted her, and towards whom she did not know she was so violently attracted, came to the house every day.

Several days had passed in this way, in a disingenuous truce to our disagreements and our passions—a truce selfishly intended by me in order that I might bring my work to an end, and which had merely served to sharpen the disagreements and bring the passions to a head. After three weeks my work had been finished, but, during the same period, my wife had—perhaps without realizing it —reached the extreme limit of her confused, obscure desire. My expedition to the town had then been all that was needed to make her see the true nature of her first disdain for the barber.

Antonio had arrived, had failed to find me; somehow or other they had met, on the stairs or in the study; perhaps he had made violent advances to her, or perhaps she had taken the initiative. Anyhow, there had been an understanding, a sudden, complete, final understanding. From that moment onwards Leda's behaviour had been characterized by the inflexibility, the velocity, the weight, of a stone that plunges through space to the bottom of a deep ravine. With a cruelty that was perhaps not unconscious, she had made an appointment with Antonio at that same place at which, the night before, I had tried to make love to her. After Antonio had gone, she had acted with cold and brutal determination, without scruples either of delicacy, of caution, or even of ordinary good taste, just as an enemy might act, not a wife who still loves her husband. She had made sure that I should be working that night when she went to her appointment, and she had played with me like a cat with a mouse in telling me that tale of her adventure with the Alpini officer, obviously suggested by her meeting with Antonio that morning. When evening came she had taken care, in dressing, not to put on the American elastic belt, so as to be more expeditious, more naked, more tempting. While I was eating she had made no attempt to conceal her own harsh impatience, disdaining even to have recourse to the hypocrisy which, in such cases, implies a homage, if not to virtue, at least to good manners. It had needed all my blindness not to see that her lack of appetite was due to that other appetite, so far more masterful. But, fearing that I should take her pretended indisposition too seriously and might even wish to keep her company in her room, she had explained it, cynically, by letting me suppose it was her monthly disorder. While I shut myself up to write in my study, she had been sitting downstairs for three hours, smoking one cigarette after another, counting the minutes and the seconds. When the time came, she had run to her appointment; and that kind of dance, at which I had been a spectator, had been simply the final explosion of the powerful too-long-repressed mechanism of her lust.

I must state, at this point, that I recognized in the whole of Leda's behaviour the deceitful yet transitory resoluteness of actions that break suddenly out from the buried places of the consciousness and are then re-absorbed, like rivers in the desert. I recognized, in other words, in these actions the furious but short-lived impetus of the involuntary infraction of an acknowledged rule. All that had happened between her and Antonio had not affected in the slightest degree her relations with me. Her intrigue with the barber—which, in all probability, would not survive that night—and her ties with me, of a year's duration, were two different things, on two entirely different planes. I was sure that, if I said nothing, Leda would go on loving me as in the past, and perhaps more; and that she herself would take steps to get rid of Antonio next day, even if she had not already done so. But this thought, far from comforting me as it should have done, depressed me even more. It was one more proof of my incapacity, of my feebleness, my impotence. To me, both creative art and my wife were granted only through pity, through affection, benevolence, reasoned goodwill; the fruits of this concession would never be either love or poetry, but merely a process of forced, decorous composition, a tepid, chaste felicity. Not for me the true masterpiece, not for me the dance on the threshing-floor. I was relegated, for ever, to mediocrity.

Meanwhile, still carried along by my grief as though by a wind, I had crossed the park, I had entered the house, I had mounted the stairs, I had returned to my task. There I sat, pen in hand, in front of a sheet of paper at the top of which I had written: "Dearest Leda." It was the letter of final and absolute farewell to my wife. Then I realized that I was weeping.

I do not know how much I wept; I only know that I wept and wrote at the same time, and that, as I wrote, the tears fell upon the words and blotted them out. I wanted to tell her that all was over between us two and that it was better for us to part, but as I thought and wrote down these things, I felt a violent pain and, as it were, a refusal on the part of my whole body, which seemed to express itself in this uninterrupted flood of tears. I realized that I was closely tied to her, that it did not in the least matter to me that she had betrayed me, and that, in the long run, it did not matter to me even if she gave herself to others for love and reserved, for me, nothing but simple affection. I tried to imagine, at moments, what life would be like without her, and I knew that, after having for so many years thought of suicide, I should really kill myself this time. Nevertheless I went on writing and weeping. And so I finished the letter and signed it. But, when I started reading it over, I saw that it was all blotted out by tears and I knew I should never have the courage to send it.

At that moment I had an exact perception of the weakness of my own character, made up, as it was, of impotence and morbidity and selfishness; and I accepted it completely, all at once. I knew that, after that night, I should be a much more modest man, and that perhaps, if I so wished, I should be able, if not exactly to change, at least to correct, myself, since in that one single night I had learned more about myself than in all the other years of my life. This thought calmed me. I rose from the desk, went into my bedroom and bathed my red, swollen eyes. Then I went back into the study and stood at the window that looked out to the front of the house.

I stood there for about ten minutes, thinking of nothing and allowing the silence and serenity of the night to calm the tumult of my spirit. I was not thinking about Leda, and was surprised when I saw her suddenly appear at one corner of the open space and run towards the door. In order to move more speedily, she was holding up, with both hands, her long dress; and, seen like that from above, as she darted across the moonlit gravel, she made me think of some little wild animal, a fox or a weasel, which, furtive, innocent, its coat still stained with blood, scurries back to its lair after a raid on a chicken-run. This sensation was so strong that I almost seemed to see her transformed into an animal, and I was conscious, for one moment, of that look of innocence as of a physical quality —almost like some wild odour. And, in spite of myself, I could not help smiling affectionately. Then, still running, she raised her eyes towards me as I stood at the window. Her eyes met mine, and I thought I detected in hers a presentiment of an unpleasant scene. She lowered her head immediately and went into the house. Slowly I drew back from the window, and went and sat down on the sofa.

16

A MOMENT later the door opened and she swept in. I recognized, in this aggressiveness of hers, a defensive move, and I could not help smiling again. Still holding the door-handle, she asked: "What are you doing—aren't you working?"

Without raising my head, I answered: "No."

"I went for a stroll in the park, as I couldn't sleep," she said, providing me with an explanation which I had not asked for; "but what's the matter with you?"

In the meantime she had walked towards the desk. But clearly she did not dare to come any nearer to me. Standing upright beside the desk, she looked at the scattered papers. I went on, with an effort: "This evening I made a discovery—a decisive discovery . . . which is going to have an important effect on my life."

I looked at her. Still standing beside the desk, she was staring at the typewriter, frowning, and with a fixed, angry look. In a loud voice she asked: "What discovery?"

So she was preparing to answer me back, I found myself thinking. Her attitude reminded me of that of certain insects, which, in danger, rise threateningly on their hind feet—an attitude which is called by naturalists the "spectral" attitude. I seemed to hear her voice shouting: "Yes, I gave myself to the barber, I *like* the barber. . . . Well, now you know; do what you like." I sighed and went on: "I discovered, when I read over my story, that it's quite worthless and that I shall never be a writer."

I saw her standing there, still and silent, and with an air

of incredulity at the sound of words so different from those she expected. Then, with a note of violence still lingering in her voice, she exclaimed: "Whatever d'you mean?"

"I'm telling you the truth," I replied calmly; "I was deceiving myself. . . . While I was writing the story it seemed to me a masterpiece, but it's really an abortion . . . and I'm nothing but a hopelessly mediocre person."

She passed her hand across her forehead and then came slowly and sat down beside me. It was clear that she was making an effort to take over the unexpected, difficult role that was being forced upon her; and that she had the utmost difficulty in doing so. "But, Silvio," she said, "how can that be possible? You were so certain."

"Now I'm certain of the exact opposite," I answered, "so much so that for a moment I almost thought of killing myself."

As I said this I raised my eyes and looked at her. And then I realized that, the whole time, even while I had been talking about my story, I had been thinking of her. Little did it matter to me, now, that the story was bad; but I could not help feeling a sharp stab of pain when I noticed the traces of her affair with Antonio which were visible all over her. Her hair was disordered, its curls loosened, and I thought I could even see a few straws still sticking in it. The bunch of flowers was no longer there; it had presumably been left on the threshing-floor. Her mouth was pale and discoloured, but with a few smears of lipstick here and there which gave her whole face a battered and distorted look. Her dress, too, was crumpled; and at the height of the knee there was a fresh stain of earth, produced, apparently, by a fall.

I realized that she knew she was in this state and that she had acted deliberately in appearing as she was. Otherwise she could easily have gone first to her room and cleaned herself up, touched up her face, taken off her dress and put on a dressing-gown. At this thought I felt a fresh spasm of pain, being confronted, as it seemed, with an arrogant and ruthless hostility. She was saying, in the meantime: "Kill yourself? Why, you're crazy . . . and all for a story that didn't turn out right."

I translated this, mentally, into: "All for one moment of aberration . . . because I couldn't resist a passing temptation." And I said: "For me this story was extremely important. . . . I know I'm a failure now . . . and I have the proof of it—in this manuscript"; and as I said it I made a brusque, almost involuntary gesture, pointing not in the direction of the desk upon which the manuscript lay, but towards her.

This time she understood (or perhaps she had already understood but had hoped to deceive me), and she lowered her eyes in a kind of confusion. The hand that she held in her lap moved downwards to her knee in order to hide the earthy stain. Bodily love is exhausting, and there are certain pretences which depend, for their efficacy, upon a physical impetus. At that moment, hampered by weariness of the senses and by her outward disorder, she must certainly have found it very difficult to recover herself and play her usual part as an affectionate wife. I feared some inept remark and said to myself that this time I would tell her the truth. Then I heard her voice, unexpectedly tremulous, asking: "Why a failure? You didn't think of me, then?"

I dwelt for a moment upon the feeling of surprise that these words gave me. There was more in her question than mere audacity and slyness—admirable, possibly, but only as a flash of unwonted smartness; there was—or so it seemed to me—a touching sincerity. I asked, in turn: "And what can you do for me? You can't possibly give me the talent that I lack."

"No," she said, in the sensible, ingenuous way she sometimes had, "but I love you."

She put out her hand towards me, seeking mine, and gazing at me all the time with those eyes of hers which seemed to become steadily clearer and more luminous as her feeling for me regained its strength and dispelled her recent excitement. I took her hand, kissed it, and fell on my knees in front of her. "I love you too," I said softly, "and by now you ought to know it . . . but I'm afraid that isn't enough to keep me alive."

I kept my face pressed against those legs which, a short time before, I had seen, naked, executing the dance of desire on the threshing-floor. Meanwhile I was pondering over the meaning of her words. And this is what I gathered from them: "I have done wrong, because I was led astray by desire . . . but I love you, and that's the only thing that counts for me. . . . I am sorry and I won't do it again."

And so everything was as I had foreseen. But now I no longer felt inclined to reject that affection of hers, however insufficient it might be. I heard her saying: "When these fits of despair come over you, you must try and think of me. . . . After all, we love each other, and that has some importance."

"Think of you?" I answered softly. "And do you think of me?"

"Always."

I said to myself that she was ~‾ ‾g. Probably she did think of me always and h‾   of me always—even when, a short time ago, she had given herself to Antonio at the threshing-floor. I might have found a certain absurdity in the way she thought of me, so constant, so ineffective, which not merely had not prevented her from betraying me, but which—as does indeed happen—had perhaps made her betrayal actually more alluring and richer in flavour. But I preferred to tell myself that she really did think of me all the time as one thinks of an unsolved and yet vital question which lies at the centre of one's more creditable preoccupations. Her thought was dictated, perhaps, by goodwill; but it suited me to think that, apart from goodwill, everything in her was dark and confused, and predisposed her to give way to temptations of the kind that had thrown her into Antonio's arms. And so it was that we were speaking different languages: I gave no importance at all to goodwill—which was made up, it seemed to me, merely of reasoning and common sense—but a great deal, on the other hand, to instinct, without which I considered that there could be neither love nor art; whereas she placed a high value upon this goodwill, which evidently appeared to her to be the best part of herself, and rejected instinct as being both wrong and inadequate. I reflected that one always loves the thing one does not possess: she, full of confused instinct, had perforce to respect clear reason, whereas I, full of bloodless reason, was naturally attracted by the richness of instinct. I found myself murmuring: "And art? Can art be created by goodwill?"

She was stroking my head and certainly did not hear those words of mine, spoken, as they were, in a very low voice; but, just as though she had heard them, she went on, a moment later, in a lively, self-possessed, affectionate voice: "Come on, get up. . . . And d'you know what we'll do now? I'll go and undress and get into bed, and then you can come and read me your story. . . . We'll see whether it's really so bad."

She rose as she spoke, with a brisk movement of her whole body. I rose too, feeling dazed and protesting that it was not worth the trouble, that there was no doubt that the story was bad and there was nothing to be done about it. But she stopped me, putting her hand to my mouth and exclaiming: "Now, come along . . . it's too early to tell yet. . . . Now I'm going to my room and you can join me there in a few minutes." Before I could speak, she had gone out.

When I was alone, I went to the desk and automatically took up the manuscript. And so, I thought, her goodwill was growing in strength and there was no doubt that she was sincere. Could I hope that this goodwill would triumph over the next temptation? I knew that only the future could answer that question for me.

I lit a cigarette and stood motionless, smoking, beside the desk. When I thought a long enough time had passed, I left the room, the manuscript under my arm, and went and knocked at her door. She at once called out to me, in a cheerful sing-song voice, to come in.

She was already in bed, sitting upright, in a magnificent

nightdress adorned with openwork and lace. The room was in darkness except for the head of the bed, upon which fell the light of the bedside lamp. She was leaning against the pillows, her arms stretched out on the sheet in front of her, with a welcoming, expectant air. Her face was exquisitely made up, all her curls were in place, and there was a new bunch of fresh flowers above her left temple. She was very beautiful: and upon her face lay that sparkling mysterious serenity in which her beauty seemed, above all, to consist. I was astonished, as I looked at her, at the thought that that face, now so calm and luminous, could have been distorted, a short time before, into that hectic grimace of lust. Smiling, she said: "Cheer up! You see I've put on my best nightie to listen to you."

I sat down, slantwise, on the edge of the bed, and said: "I'm reading it to you only because you want me to. . . . I've already told you it's bad."

"Never mind. . . . Come on. I'm listening."

I took up the first page and began reading. I read the whole story straight through without stopping, merely casting a glance at her, now and then, as she listened seriously and attentively. As I read I was confirmed in my former opinion: the thing was respectable, and that was all. Nevertheless this "respectability" which, not long before, had seemed to me a characteristic which had no importance, now—I do not know why—appeared to have more weight than I had imagined. This less unfavourable impression, however, did not distract my mind from its main preoccupation, which was my wife. I was wondering all the time what she would say at the end of the reading. There seemed to me to be two courses open to her: the first consisted in exclaiming immediately: "But, Silvio, what do you mean, it's very fine indeed"; the second, in admitting that the story was mediocre. The first was the way of indifference and deceit. By giving me to understand that the story was good when she thought it was not (and she could not but think so), she would be showing clearly that she wished to lead me by the nose, and that between her and me there could be a relationship merely of falsity and pity. The second was the way of love, even if it was only a love like hers, made up of goodwill and affection. I wondered, not without anxiety, which way she would choose. If she said that the story was good, I had made up my mind to cry: "The story's bad and you're nothing but a whore!"

I read through the whole story with this idea in mind, and, the nearer I drew towards the end, the more I slowed down the pace of my reading, being fearful of what would happen. Finally I read the last sentence, and then said: "That's all," raising my eyes towards her.

We looked at each other in silence; and, like a passing cloud in a clear sky, I saw a shadow of deceit spread, for one moment, over her face. For one moment, certainly, she thought of lying to me, of crying out that the story was good and thus revealing herself in all her coldness and cunning and in the act of administering the false comfort of a pitying flattery. But this shadow vanished almost at once; and it seemed to be replaced by a love for me which consisted, first of all, in truth towards me and respect for me. In a voice full of a sincere disappointment, she said: "Perhaps you're right. . . . It isn't the masterpiece you thought. . . . But neither is it as bad as you think now. It's interesting to listen to."

Greatly relieved, I answered almost joyfully: "Didn't I tell you so?"

"It's very well written," she went on.

"It's not enough, to write well."

"But perhaps," she said, "perhaps you haven't worked at it enough. . . . If you re-wrote it—more than once, if necessary—in the end it would be just as you want it to be."

She was thinking, then, that in art too, goodwill was of greater value than the gifts of instinct. "But I want it to be," I said, "exactly as inspiration produces it—or lack of inspiration. . . . And if there isn't inspiration it's not worth while working and worrying at it."

"That's just where you're wrong," she exclaimed with animation. "You don't give enough importance to work and worry . . . but really they're extremely important. That's the way things get done—they don't just happen, as though by a miracle."

We went on arguing for some time, both of us firm in our own very different points of view. Finally I folded the manuscript in four and thrust it into my pocket, saying: "Well, well, don't let's talk about it any more."

There was a moment's silence. Then I said softly: "You don't mind having an unsuccessful writer for a husband?"

She answered at once: "I've never thought of you as a writer."

"How have you thought of me, then?"

"Well, I don't know," she said, smiling. "How can I possibly say? I know you too well by now. . . . I know just what you're like. . . . You're the same for me, always —whether you write or don't write."

"But if you had to pronounce an opinion, what would it be?"

She hesitated, and then said, with sincerity: "But one can't pronounce an opinion when one loves."

And so we always came back again to the same point. There was, in this protestation of hers that she loved me, a touching persistence that moved me deeply. I took her hand and said: "You're right. . . . And I too, just because I love you, although I know you very well, couldn't pass judgment upon you."

With a flash of intelligence in her eyes, she exclaimed: "It is so, isn't it? When one loves someone, one loves every aspect of that person—defects and all."

I should have liked to say to her at that moment, with perfect sincerity: "I love you as you are now, sitting up in bed, calm and serene in your beautiful nightdress, with your curls and your bunch of flowers and your clear, shining eyes. And I love you as you were a little time ago when you were dancing the dance of desire and gnashing your teeth and pulling up your dress and clinging to Antonio. . . . And I shall love you always." But I said nothing of all this, because I realized that she understood that I knew everything and that everything was now settled between us. Instead, I said: "Perhaps one day I'll rewrite the story . . . it's not finished with yet. . . . Some day, when I think I'm capable of expressing certain things."

"I'm convinced too," she said cheerfully, "that you ought to rewrite it—after some time."

I kissed her good-night and went off to bed. I slept extremely well, with a deep, harsh sleep like the sleep of a child who has been beaten by its parents for some fault or caprice, and has screamed and wept a great deal and then, finally, been forgiven. Next morning I rose late, shaved myself and, after breakfast, suggested to my wife that we should go for a walk before lunch. She agreed and we went out together.

A little beyond the farm buildings, on the top of another mound, were the ruins of a small church. We climbed up to it by a mule-track and sat down on the low wall that ran round the churchyard, in full view of the vast panorama. The church was of great antiquity, as could be seen from the Romanesque capitals of the two pillars supporting the exterior porch. Apart from this porch, nothing was left but a portion of the walls, a fallen apse and the almost unrecognizable stump of a tower. The churchyard, paved with old grey stones, was all grass-grown, and beneath the little porch one could catch a glimpse, through the cracks in the gaping boards of the rustic door, of the rampant bushes, their foliage gleaming in the sunshine, that ran riot in the apse. Then, as I looked at the church, I noticed that there was a face or mask carved on one of the capitals. Time had worn and smoothed away the sculpture, which must have always been rather rudimentary and now seemed almost formless; not so much so, however, that one could not distinguish the sinister face of a demon such as the sculptors of those days were in the habit of portraying in church bas-reliefs for the admonishment of the faithful. I was suddenly struck by a remote resemblance between this ancient, half-effaced grin and the grimace that I had seen upon my wife's face the previous night.

Yes, it was the same grimace, and that stonemason of bygone times had certainly intended, by stressing the mournful sensuality of the heavy lips and the feverish, greedy expression in the eyes, to suggest the same kind of temptation. I turned my eyes from the capital and looked at Leda. She was gazing at the view and appeared to be meditating. Then she turned towards me and said: "Listen. . . . I was thinking last night about your story. . . . I believe I know why it's not convincing."

"Why?"

"You meant to represent yourself and me, didn't you?"

"Yes, to a certain extent."

"Well, your facts were wrong, to start with. . . . What I mean is, one feels that when you wrote the story you didn't know me well enough, nor yourself either. . . . Perhaps it was too soon to talk about us two and our relationship . . . particularly about me; you haven't shown me as I really am. . . . You've idealized me too much."

"Anything else?"

"No, nothing else. . . . I think that, after some time, when we know each other better, you must take up the story again, as you said last night. . . . I'm sure you'll make something good out of it."

I said nothing; all I did was to stroke her hand. And, as I did this, I was looking over her shoulder at the capital with the demon's face on it and thinking that, in order to take up the story again, I should have not merely to know the devil as well as the unknown stonemason had known him, but also to know his opposite. "It'll take a long time," I said softly, finishing my thought aloud.